The Spirits of Ireland

Raymond Peter Foley

The Spirits of Ireland

Cover and Graphics by William Raymond Miller

Printed in The United State of America

First Printing March 1998
10 9 8 7 6 5 4 3 2 1

Copyright 1998 by Raymond Peter Foley

Published by FOLEY Books, Inc.

ISBN 0 - 9617655 - 4 - 2

Dedication To

John J. Foley, Sr. (Limerick)
and
Ellen Josephine (Russell) Foley (Tipperary)
and
Ryan Peter Foley
a great Irish American

The Spirits of Ireland

The Spirits of Ireland

Acknowledgment

To all the suppliers who came forth with
information on their products:

IDV North America
Nancy Larkin, Camelot
Vince Piscopo, Wells, Rich, Greene
Stephen Davis, Heineken USA
John Vidal, Anita Galvin, Brown-Forman Beverage Co.
Alan Lewis, C&C International, Ltd.
William J. Walsh, A. Hardy USA/Ltd.
Patricia Bornmann, Whitehall Advertising
Michael L. Avitable, Marie Brizard Wines & Spirits USA
Meg Syberg, David Sherman Corp.
Howard Pulchin, Guinness Import Company
Barry Berish, Michael Donahue, Jim Beam Brands Co.
Jim Cotter, Stephen L. Kauffman, Susan Overton, Heaven Hill
Distilleries, Inc.
Katie Bush, Keith Steer, Halbleib/Beggs, Inc.
Mark Doyle, Austin, Nichols & Co., Inc.
The Milton Samuels Agency
Karen Danik, Cairns & Associates, Inc.

Plus, Jaclyn Wilson Foley for her loyalty, Loretta Natiello for
being my best friend, J.K. for his assistance, and all the great
Irish bars and bartenders who contributed to BARTENDER
Magazine with their wonderful recipes.

The Spirits of Ireland

Index

Introduction

God gave the recipe for whiskey to the people of Ireland because he loved them. Among His treasures are a few that are exceedingly rare, and one of these is the Water of Life. "What better gift," He asked Himself one fine misty morning, "for these truly unusual and gifted people?" No wonder they call it spirit.

In his customary oblique manner, the Almighty did not simply appear by a Sligo bog one day with barley under one arm and an alembic under the other. He chose instead to instruct folk in a distant land — hazy references mention "the East," probably lands occupied by the Mohammedans — in the art of distillation. The stimulant of choice among these folk was coffee, and they never tried their hand at distilling grains. Theirs is the loss; they chose instead to distill fragrances.

It could have been any monk, or group of monks, but some of the old folk insist it was St. Patrick who pocketed the formula for distillation on a visit to "the East" and returned with it to the Emerald Isle in the 5th Century. Born in Britain, Patrick was captured and taken to Ireland as a slave at age 16. He escaped six years later, wandered around the Continent, and eventually took holy orders. The record of his visit to "the East" is missing, but he might have been among those Christians who traveled to the land of the infidel to spread the gospel. In any event, he returned to Ireland, thrust himself and the teachings of the Roman church upon the king at Tara, gave the snakes their marching orders, and set up the first pot still. What a day!

It is impossible to imagine what the aqua vitae of ancient Ireland tasted like. Doubtless, the quality of the grains was high, but they had no idea what yeast was; perhaps the early distillers saved some yeast from the foam of the mash, an early stage of the whiskey-making process, or else they relied on wild, airborne yeast. It is probable that the first distillers also consumed their whiskey soon after distillation. The idea of aging in wood no doubt came after years of experimentation.

Whiskey history is obscure, but we know two things for sure: It was a volatile and impure liquor, but it had (and has) medicinal qualities.

The value of aqua vitae as a benefit to human health was unquestioned. The quality of food and water throughout the world was always in question. Distillation, therefore, was a purification of matter, a transformation into spiritual state of the ordinary. A draught of the spirit could negate the impurities ingested into the body during the normal course of a meal. It was considered also to be a restorative, a remedy for sickness. We know this from our grandmothers, yet the government of this country seeks to quell all knowledge of this common and delightful cure.

The other certainty was this: The high concentration of impurities in homemade whiskey had the potential to impart a ferocious headache and a stupendous hangover. No wonder the Irish have a predilection for cabbage. That vegetable is one of the few on earth that contains a compound said to alleviate the discomfort encountered on the morning after an evening of insobriety.

St. Patrick's legacy was a nation steeped in Catholic tradition and study. So renowned was Ireland for its religious scholarship that it attracted priests and monks from all Christendom.

In most of the European lands dotted with monasteries, the men who took holy orders also took to making beer, wine and spirits. It was the Irish brothers, therefore, who slowly refined the art of distillation, thereby refining the whiskey itself.

Make no mistake: The Irish were the world's first distillers of spirits. This is not to denigrate anything Scottish; the Scotch whisky experience is as complex and rewarding as that of Irish whiskey. But, be it known that the people of Ireland were distilling whiskey at a time when the Picts, the predecessors of the Scots (who came from Ireland in the first place), were still smearing their bodies with blue paint and stealing cattle in the Lowlands.

Much of the history of Ireland contains events unpleasant and disappointing to the Irish, which is yet another reason God gave them the whiskey, so that they could endure strife. It was one such unpleasantness that gave the outside world its first taste of the Water of Life. In the 1100s, King Henry II of England sent his soldiers west to invade Hibernia, the first of many unwelcome visits by the Crown. They burned and looted and inflicted the usual pain on the Irish people, but they also discovered that the locals enjoyed something they called uisge beatha. The British soldiers were not cunning linguists and could not properly mouth the Gaelic, so they bastardized the first word a few times and, eventually, it came to be pronounced "whiskey." They discovered also that they enjoyed drinking it and brought some home with them to the delight of their countrymen and even became promoters of this saintly liquor on their travels around the globe.

The rest of the history of Irish whiskey reads just like the history of the rest of the world: the efforts of government to suck taxes out of the people. By the 1500s, the government in Ireland was English, and England was ever in search of sources of revenue with which to support its imperialistic expansion. Levying of punitive laws and fees on illicit stills and distillers, and even on raw materials used in making whiskey, increased over the next several centuries. The stills went underground, out into the bogs, ever farther from the eye and reach of the exciseman. It is safe to say that every village, and many a farmstead, had an operating still. The "poitin" was often wicked — clear spirit, unaged, impure, highly alcoholic, but satisfying to the rebellious Irish soul.

In 1608, in County Antrim in what is now Northern Ireland, the first legal distillery was born on the banks of the river Bush. The fact that it was called "Old Bushmills Distillery" gives ample indication that the making of whiskey had gone on for some time in the village of Bushmills. It is told that in 1276, Sir

Robert Savage, the local landlord, fortified his troops with uisge beatha before they took to battle. The 1608 license was granted to Sir Thomas Phillips by King James I, and the whiskey soon became a favorite among the nobles of London society. Its popularity spread and, within the next two centuries, the whiskey made at Old Bushmills became a favorite in the Western Hemisphere to the extent that most of the distillery's product was exported.

Fire destroyed the Old Bushmills Distillery in 1885, gutting all but one building. The loss was devastating. But the world needs whiskey, and the entire complex was rebuilt and operating within three years. In 1897, the distillery announced a special issue for Queen Victoria's Diamond Jubilee: 10,000 bottles of its Pure Old Malt Whiskey.

Two other great Irish distilleries were established in Dublin, Ireland's capital, in the late 18th Century: John Jameson & Son in 1780, and Sir John Power & Son in 1791. Jameson is now the best-selling Irish whiskey in the world. By the end of the 1800s, it is estimated that more than 400 registered brands of Irish whiskey were available in the United States alone.

Meanwhile, the poitin men still operated in the back country, smuggling in raw materials and smuggling out their unlicensed whiskey. The uncountable little stills in the hills and bogs gave rise to an army of excise men and, for more than a century, blood was shed on both sides over the unlicensed distillation of uisge beatha.

The quality of the whiskey 200 years ago probably was not as high as it is today, because competition among distillers was causing them to push the product out into the marketplace. Good whiskey must be made slowly and with care, but the probable coarseness of the whiskey back then was considered by the growing anti-alcohol contingent to be a contributor to the social ills. A government act in 1823 succeeded in placing strict controls on the distillation process and, while this meant more regulation and higher tariffs, it also meant a slower distillation and a whiskey of higher quality.

Booming though it was, the 19th Century saw the beginnings of a long period of difficulty for the distillers of Irish whiskey. This led to a dramatic decline in the 20th Century from which the whiskey's popularity has barely emerged. Though production remained high in the 1800s, several factors combined to start the slide. The continuous increase in duties on spirits was only one of them.

Another was competition from other intoxicating beverages.

Rum was a force to contend with, both in England and in the Americas. Cognac and other brandies were making inroads, and wine was well established in Britain. A third factor was famine. Nothing drove the Irish people from their homeland the way the potato famines did. Couple that with the evictions from their native soil by the landlords and it is not surprising that, in 1847, more than 200,000 Irish left the island. Within a few years emigration was more than a quarter million a year.

But the greatest of threats to pot-distilled Irish whiskey was homegrown, born in the mind of Aeneas Coffey of Dublin. For many years, Coffey had been an excise man, rising eventually to become Inspector General of Excise. After he resigned from government service in 1824, he put his wits to work and invented what became known as the Coffey still. This remarkable invention allowed for continuous production of grain spirit that was just shy of pure alcohol. It remains nearly unchanged in design to this day.

The Coffey still incensed and disgusted the Irish whiskey distillers. The big companies rejected it as an adulteration. But across the water in Scotland and England, the continuous still found a home. Soon the production of grain whiskey began to flood the market of the empire, but what was most offensive to the pot-whiskey distillers was that the grain spirit was being blended with a small amount of pure Irish whiskey and sold, both abroad and at home, as the real thing. Elsewhere in the British Empire, blended Scotch whisky began its long rise in popularity, further dampening sales of the Irish product.

For more than half a century, the Irish distillers and their supporters fought against the blenders. Even doctors came out on the side of the pot distillers, railing in professional journals against health risks from consumption of "fermented liquor... made from damaged grain, rotten potatoes, refuse molasses or other waste." The cause in favor of whiskey purity was joined also by some distillers of fine Scotch, who saw the blending craze diminish their business as well.

Though the traditional distillers never won the blending war, two laws were set down in the first part of the 20th Century that gave some benefit to the distillers and consumers of fine whiskey. The first was that, henceforth, Irish whiskey can be made only in Ireland, and that Scotch whisky could be made only in Scotland. The second was that all whiskey, whether distilled in the old copper alembics or in the Coffey contraption, must mature for a minimum of three years in wood. The Coffey still people didn't like that much, for it set back their production three years, but the result was — and is — a much better whiskey.

The early years of the 20th Century brought Ireland its independence from England (1916), but not without great cost. The 1919 partitioning of Ireland into north and south gave rise to two years of civil war, followed by economic war: England and Ireland closed its markets to each other. That shut off sales of Irish whiskey to Canada, Australia, a great deal of Africa, India, New Zealand, parts of the Far East, and parts of the Caribbean. It is estimated that Irish whiskey sales in the British Empire amounted to 25 percent of the whole business. That nice slice of the economic pie went to Scotch whisky.

As if that wasn't enough, the silly government on the other side of the Atlantic shut off the legal trade in liquor for 14 long years, something they called Prohibition, which turned out to have done more harm than good, both in the U.S. and abroad. Bootleggers had a picnic, and went so far as to promote inferior products as "Irish Whiskey," which damaged the reputation of the real thing. And when Prohibition ended in 1934, the producers of Irish whiskey did not have enough product on hand to re-enter the U.S. market at once. Whiskey takes a long time to mature. Stocks were low, and the Irish suffered again.

Irish whiskey languished, and the number of distilleries gradually shrunk to a handful. But along comes a trade endeavor to stir sales. Between 1966 and 1972, the remaining five distilleries formed the Irish Distillers Group, aiming at revitalizing the global market for the original Water of Life.

Since 1987, old distilleries have reopened and new distillers are being opened as we write. New blends and many more new and exciting products are coming from this great land - Ireland.

Today we are comfortable with blended whiskey, with the single malts, with the assurance that we can buy and savor fine Irish whiskey, the best that Ireland has to offer. The Divine Distiller has done, and continues to do, His part in blessing us with Irish whiskey. The Irish, with their music and their stories and poetry, have conquered our hearts, and with their uisge beatha they have banished our thirst.

I hope the following pages of information will help you enjoy the spirits of Ireland.

Slainte!

Irish Whiskey —
A Little Bit Of Information

Bushmills

The "Old Bushmills" Distillery in County Antrim, Ireland is located in the heart of a lush barley-growing area and along the banks of St. Columb's Rill, a tributary of the River Bush.

The oldest licensed distillery in the world, the "Old Bushmills" Distillery was founded in 1608, but even before that date there was evidence of magic in the air: In 1276, Sir Robert Savage, ground landlord of Bushmills, fortified his troops before battle with "a mighty drop of aquavitae."

The "Old Bushmills" Distillery has always used the agricultural riches surrounding it to produce a very special spirit —

and today it is the birthplace of four distinctive whiskeys: Bushmills Premium Irish Whiskey, Black Bush Special Irish Whiskey, Bushmills Single Malt Irish Whiskey 10 Years Old and Bushmills Rare Single Irish Malt Whiskey 16 Years Old, a single malt Irish whiskey finished in three different woods.

Like its production process, Bushmills' ingredients have stayed the same over the centuries. First there is barley, which is examined, graded and cleansed to perfection as malt. The malt is then dried in a closed kiln kept separate from smoke; exposure of the barley to heat brings a special smoothness to the spirit.

After the malt has mellowed for several weeks, it is milled into grist. The grist is mixed with water from St. Columb's Rill at various temperatures and yeast is added to the resulting mixture. Because the river flows over beds of basalt, the water imparts a unique sweet flavor to the distilled spirit.

All whiskeys produced at the "Old Bushmills" Distillery are distilled three times in authentic copper pot stills. The primary and secondary distillations remove impurities, while the third distillation helps create a smoother, cleaner spirit and ensures the quality of the whiskey.

Bushmills Premium Irish Whiskey

The original and best-known whiskey from the "Old Bushmills" Distillery is Bushmills Premium Irish Whiskey. Malt whiskey reserved for Bushmills is aged seven years in oak casks especially selected to bring out the light, delicate characteristics of the whiskey. When mature, this malt whiskey is blended with a single Irish grain that has a light aroma and hint of sweetness. The result is golden in color, smooth in texture and delicate in flavor.

Black Bush Special Irish Whiskey

Black Bush Special Irish Whiskey is a rich, dark blend that is comprised of a high percentage of pure malt whiskey. Malt whiskey that becomes Black Bush is aged nine to eleven years in selected sherry-seasoned oak casks before being blended with a small portion of a special single grain whiskey to enhance the character of the malt.

The combination is then returned to the cask for "marrying." As the whiskeys mellow together, producing a uniquely rounded bouquet and rich amber hue, the distinctive taste of Black Bush is born.

Bushmills Single Malt Irish Whiskey 10 Years Old

Possessing a warm, sweet aroma and well-balanced flavor, Bushmills Malt is a delicate whiskey crafted from 100 percent malted barley.

The malt used to make Bushmills Malt is deliberately dried in closed kilns. This prevents the malt from absorbing the fire's smokiness (hence, no smoky flavors are imparted to the final distilled spirit), while still retaining the character of the malt.

Unlike its brethren Bushmills Irish Whiskey and Black Bush, Bushmills Malt is a single whiskey that, after aging 10 years, finds its full flavor, character and dark, rich hue. A blender's skills are never needed to enhance Bushmills Malt; its flavor and character evolve naturally over time in the carefully selected American bourbon oak casks in which it is aged.

Bushmills Rare Single Malt Irish Whiskey 16 Years Old

Bushmills Malt 16 Years Old is a single malt Irish whiskey finished in three different woods for unparalleled taste quality.

Unlike any other Irish single malt whiskey, Bushmills Malt 16 Years Old is finished in bourbon, sherry and port woods. To the already clean, non-smoky taste of fine Bushmills Irish whiskey, the woods add elements of depth and flavor. The result is a rich, smooth old malt with a wonderful complexity of sweet, spicy and woody flavors.

Connemara

Pot Still Peated Single Malt Irish Whiskey

The Connemara Pot Stilled Peated Single Malt is a unique product, being the only Peated Single Malt on the market.

It's name, Connemara, hails from the famous Connemara region in the west of Ireland. A region of wild beauty, with majestic mountains, soft rain, mist, lakes and pure water carried eastwards by the Atlantic winds.

The Connemara Pot Stilled Peated Single Malt captures the natural beauty of this majestic region of peated lands and mountains.

The mash of pure clear spring water and peated malted barley gives the Connemara its unique and distinctive flavors. The natural ingredients and traditional distilling methods are employed to create a whiskey which, after slowly maturing for long years in oak casks, is simply unique.

The secret of the Connemara's special peated taste is in the drying process where the newly germinated malted barley is dried over a peat fire with smoke rising through it to add a famed and distinctive peaty flavor and aroma.

Connemara Tasting Notes

Nose: Intense peatiness for an Irish whiskey yet less smoky than an Islay, with a heathery bouquet and inklings of honey.

Taste: The sweetness of honey and spices gradually gives way to a smooth rise in the peated malt flavor, a good balance is struck with neither being overpowering.

Finish: The honey diffuses in the mouth as the peat lingers on. There is a delicate taste of vanilla and a sense of the matured oak. Intricate and amazing.

Comment: Unique in being Ireland's only peated malt, this is a mature, top class peat whiskey with a bright future.

John Jameson

In the 18th century, Dublin was the Second City of the British Empire and the seventh largest city in the world. Irish Whiskey had already acquired a reputation for greatness, but among Irish whiskeys, the Dublin whiskeys were particularly prized and, during the latter half of the 18th century, many famous distilleries were founded in Ireland's capital.

Among them was John Jameson. In 1780, during the golden age of Irish Whiskey, Jameson founded his distillery in Bow Street near to the heart of Dublin. He quickly acquired a reputation for making the finest Irish Whiskey in the world, a position Jameson still has today.

Jameson 1780 12 year old Irish whiskey is the direct descendant of the liqueur whiskey which confounded Monsieur Hennessy in the 1920s, and will confound experts as surely in the 1990s. Its reputation as a digestif is as solid today as it was then and, despite the Irishman's love for brandy, a well-matured whiskey like 1780 has as sure a place as any fine cognac at the end of a good dinner.

John Jameson first established his distillery in Bow Street, Dublin in 1780. From the earliest days he committed himself to producing the finest whiskey possible. By the end of the nineteenth century, his products had established a reputation for top quality all over the world. This was partly due to his commitment to the traditional Pot Still method of distillation which continues to this day. The cheaper whiskies from Scotland were blended with substantial quantities of Column Still whiskey which, although quicker to make than Pot Still whiskey, had little flavour of their own.

Jameson Irish Whiskey is made from pure Irish water and choice native Irish barley. Part of the barley used is first malted but, unlike their cousins in Scotland who dry their malt over an open peat fire which gives a smoky flavor to the final whiskey, the distillers at Jameson dry their malt in a closed kiln, so that the smoky flavour is deliberately absent.

The art of the distiller is to separate and retain exactly those elements of the alcohol family which, when mature, will make a perfect whiskey (or brandy), and to discard those elements which are undesirable, which give a poor flavor. In John Jameson's opinion, only three separate distillations in a Pot Still will achieve this perfect balance of flavour congeners. No other whisk(e)y or brandy in the world is distilled more than twice. Thereafter, the whiskey must mature for twelve years in specially selected oak casks in dark, aromatic warehouses. During this time strange, almost magical things happen to the spirit: some of the higher alcohols evaporate through the porous oak of the cask; oxygen enters through the porous oak, and some of the natural wood extractives, called lignins, are dissolved by the spirit. It is these lignins that give the whiskey its color. Only time will complete this slow interaction called maturation. There are no short cuts in the making of a great whiskey.

Jameson is the world's largest selling Irish whiskey, and has been known worldwide for more than 200 years.

Jameson is delicious when consumed on-the-rocks as in America, with water as in Ireland, or with soda as in England. It is also excellent in cocktails, because the absence of any smoky taste makes it uniquely mixable. Consumers today are finding the smooth taste of Jameson, the original taste of whisk(e)y, particularly agreeable.

Jameson 1780

One of the most charming stories ever told about Irish Whiskey was by Maurice Healy, author of The Old Munster Circuit, in a book first published in 1940 called "stay me in Flagons."

"Many years ago Monsieur Hennessy was visiting Cork and was entertained by the hospitable Dominic Daly, one of our leading citizens, and also one engaged in the wine and spirit trade. After lunch the host said: "Would you like a liqueur with your coffee?" Monsieur Hennessy concealed a grimace, and accepted. "Bring that peculiar decanter," said Dommy Daly to his butler. A few minutes later he turned to his guest and said, "Now, tell me what this is."

"Oh," said Monsieur Hennessy, "it is very difficult to be precise in these matters, but I should call it a Grande Champagne...probably an 1893."

"It's a John Jameson Ten-Year-Old Whiskey," replied Dommy.

Jameson 1780 should be drunk as a digestif, on its own, without water, ice or soda. It should be served at room temperature in a glass that permits the nose to enjoy the aroma that rises from the spirit.

Kilbeggan Irish Whiskey

Kilbeggan Irish Whiskey is an authentic product of Ireland.

It is distilled and bottled by Cooley Distillery Plc., in Riverstown, Dundalk, County Louth, and John Licke & Co., County Westmeath, the country's oldest licensed distillery dating back to 1757. Cooley Distillery is the only independent, Irish-owned distillery remaining in Ireland.

Kilbeggan is made from a mixture of locally grown grains including barley, corn, rye, wheat and oats. Kilbeggan Irish Whiskey is an excellent quality blend of aged grain and malt whiskeys.

While Irish whiskey is a "first cousin" to Scotch whisky, it doesn't have Scotch's traditionally "smoky" taste. Kilbeggan, in fact, has a gentler, sweeter taste and a lighter finish.

The whiskey's exceptionally smooth taste is attributed in part to the lime-softened water from the nearby River Crann, which is used in making Kilbeggan.

"Kilbeggan" is Gaelic for "little church." What is now an idyllic village in the center of Ireland was, for many years, an active religious community built around a monastery. The first licensed whiskey distillery in the world was established in Kilbeggan in 1757.

Midleton
Very Rare Irish Whiskey

Midleton Very Rare is the most exclusive and prestigious whiskey ever produced in Ireland.

Midleton Very Rare, like all Irish whiskeys, is distilled three times for maximum purity, from the finest Irish barley and clear pure water. Most other whiskies are only distilled twice.

It is a blend of particularly fine distillates, matured in individually selected oak casks, in dark aromatic cellars for 10 to 15 years.

Each cask is monitored very carefully by the Master Distiller and when, in his opinion the cask has reached the point of optimal maturation, the whiskey is drawn from the cask and included in that year's release.

Midleton Very Rare is a truly handcrafted whiskey of great complexity and subtlety of flavor, to be appreciated by the connoisseur of fine spirits.

Each bottle is numbered to record ownership and individually signed by the master distiller as a final guarantee of exclusivity and outstanding quality. It is then secured in a quality ramin wood gift case.

Paddy

Named for Paddy Flaherty, a salesman for the Cork Distillers Company in the 1920s. To meet the demand of distillery-bottled Irish Whiskey, Cork Distillers sent out their best salesman, Paddy Flaherty, to make the new whiskey known throughout the area. He did so well that the customers began ordering "Paddy Flaherty's Whiskey." Cork distillers got the hint and the name "Paddy Flaherty" appeared on the bottle, later shortened to "Paddy."

Powers Irish Whiskey

In 1791, during the golden age of Irish Whiskey, James Power founded his distillery in John's Lane near the Western Gate of Dublin. He quickly acquired a reputation for making one of the finest Irish Whiskeys in the world, a position Powers still has today. When James Power died in 1817, he was succeeded by his son who became Sir John Power and High Sheriff of Dublin. John Power greatly extended the Distillery and increased the popularity of Powers Irish Whiskey at home and abroad. By 1891, the year of their first centenary, Powers was exporting extensively. They exhibited their produce at the World's Fair in Chicago in 1893 in the form of an enormous model of an Irish Round Tower made of bottles of Powers Irish Whiskey.

In 1886, John Power & Son was one of the first distillers in the world to introduce the habit of distillery bottling. Before then, whiskey — and indeed wine and beer — was delivered in oak barrels and sold "from the wood." While in the oak barrel, these drinks continued to change and were liable to contamination. To protect the quality of their good name, Powers would mature the whiskey in their own warehouses under their own control and then bottle it for sale labeled with a distinctive Gold Label. Unlike wine, whiskey stops maturing when it is bottled, and customers started to call for "the Powers with the Gold Label" because they found the quality was always reliable, always consistent. As a result, Powers became Ireland's largest selling brand of Irish whiskey, a position it still holds, and has been known around the world for 200 years.

Powers Irish Whiskey is made from pure Irish water and choice native Irish barley. Part of the barley used is first malted. Unlike their cousins in Scotland who dry their malt over an open peat fire which gives a smoky flavour to the final whisky, the distillers at Powers dry their malt in a closed kiln, so that the smoky flavor is deliberately absent.

To achieve the maximum purity of the spirit, Powers — like all Irish Whiskey — is distilled three times in huge copper pot stills. No other whiskey in the world is distilled more than twice. Finally, it is filled into oak barrels and put away to sleep for years in vast, dark aromatic warehouses. Only time can complete the magic of Powers Irish Whiskey.

The origins of Tullamore Dew Irish whiskey can be traced back to 1829 when the Tullamore Distillery was founded in Tullamore, County Offaly, situated in the heart of Ireland. The Owner was a famed distiller, Michael Molloy.

The location was well chosen - a rich agricultural and grain growing region, providing both the fine barley and pure water essential to the creation of good whiskey.

Following the deaths of Mr. Molloy, the distillery passed into the hands of the Daly family with Captain Bernard Daly in charge of the business. A keen sportsman, Captain Daly left the routine running of the distillery to one of his colleagues, Daniel E. Williams, who eventually became general manager of Tullamore.

Daniel E. Williams was the major influence on the expansion and development of the distillery and his family became joint shareholders in Tullamore with Captain Daly.

His initials, D-E-W, inspired the whiskey to be named "Tullamore Dew" with its slogan "Give every man his Dew" which is still featured on every bottle today.

Not only was Tullamore famous for its Irish whiskey but, in 1947, it also became the birthplace of Irish Mist liqueur, based on an ancient Irish recipe rediscovered by Daniel E. Williams' grandson, Desmond.

Tullamore Dew whiskey was used in the preparation of Irish Mist for many years.

For nearly 50 years the whole Irish whiskey industry was badly affected by two international events that, together, caused a serious decline in the fortunes of all the leading brands.

The first event was the USA's Prohibition period (1919-1933) during which time a major export market disappeared completely. The second was a trade war with England in the 1930s which resulted in the loss of all Irish whiskey sales in England and the British Empire — including Canada, Australia, New Zealand and parts of the Caribbean and Far East.

With the majority of Irish whiskey markets removed, the distilleries decreased their production and lowered their stockholdings of maturing whiskeys.

The final consequence of this chain of events was felt when Prohibition laws in the United States were eventually repealed. Immediately, demand was renewed - but the Irish whiskey industry had insufficient stocks to satisfy it (allowing Scotch whisky to gain a substantial position in the market).

Tullamore Dew, like many Irish whiskeys, was unable to sustain itself successfully through this difficult period. In 1965, the business was sold to Powers.

Between 1966 and 1972, all the remaining Irish distillers came together to regenerate the industry - ultimately under the name of "The Irish Distillers Group."

Production was also consolidated into two distilleries - Midleton Distillery in County Cork (where Tullamore Dew is distilled today) and the Old Bushmills Distillery in County Antrim, Northern Ireland.

The Tullamore Dew - Production

Tullamore Dew is a premium Irish whiskey - distilled, matured and vatted (blended) at the Midleton Distillery in County Cork, Ireland.

Its fine quality and distinctive taste are unique among Irish whiskeys. Connoisseurs describe Tullamore Dew's taste as "subtle, smooth and with a pleasant maltiness combined with charred wood undertones and the natural flavor of golden barley."

Tullamore Dew is also considered to have "none of the over-laying smokiness of Scotch whisky nor the sweetness of the American bourbon."

This subtle, smooth flavor is derived from the unique way in which Irish whiskey is produced.

Natural Cereal Grains

One of the most important flavor components in Irish whiskey is unmalted barley - which is distilled with malted barley in a pot still.

The malted barley is created by allowing barley to start growing in moist conditions, then stopping the growth by drying it over coal fires. This "malting" process brings out the sugars in the grain - which will later be turned into alcohol.

(The malting process itself differs from that used in Scotch. There, the grains are dried over peaty fires, giving Scotch whiskies their peaty smokiness. The absence of this is one of the defining characteristics of Irish whiskey.)

Mashing & Fermenting

The first stage in Irish whiskey production mixes hot Irish spring water with the crushed grains (known as "mashing").

The resulting sugary liquid ("wort") is collected and "fermented" by adding yeast to produce an alcoholic "wash" (with about 8.5% alcohol by volume).

Distilling

The "wash" is boiled in large copper pot stills and the vapor cooled and collected. This process is repeated to remove the harsh elements of the spirit and improve the quality of the final whiskey.

The main point of difference between Irish whiskey and other whiskies/whiskeys is that both pot still and grain whiskies are distilled three times not twice, giving a more concentrated and purer distillate.

In addition, the Irish distill their whiskey in much larger pot stills than the Scots, providing further individuality.

It is important to recognize that the distinctive character of Irish whiskey is derived from the distilling, not the blending. This is why the Irish refer to "vatting" rather than blending, to emphasize that the skill lies in creating the distillates rather than blending them later.

Maturing

The distillates (the new spirits) are matured in oak casks that have previously been used for either sherry or bourbon production. They mature for a minimum of three years - although usually for much longer.

Vatting (Blending)

As with Scotch, the flavorful pot still whiskey is blended with a lighter, more neutral grain spirit which serves to lighten the body of the final whiskey.

Blend variations are also achieved through the use of differing ages of whiskey and of different barrel types maturation - in casks previously used for sherry, rum or Bourbon, or in new oak casks.

The Tullamore Dew Blend

Tullamore Dew's particular taste character depends on the correct balance of mature whiskeys vatted together by the blender:

POT STILL WHISKEY is the most important feature and provides the foundation flavor. Starting with a mash of both malted and unmalted barley, it is distilled three times in a giant copper "still."

GRAIN WHISKEY has a simpler flavor than its pot still equivalent, being based on maize and a small proportion of malted barley. It is distilled in a continuous column still, again three times.

Tyrconnell
Single Malt Irish Whiskey

The Tyrconnell is the flagship brand of one of the oldest distilleries in Ireland. A traditional single malt, it has a fresh malty bouquet, a smooth and subtle flavor and a delicately dry finish.

The Tyrconnell Single Malt Irish Whiskey is a premium Irish whiskey made from a mash of pure malted barley produced at a single distillery—hence, the description: single malt whiskey. In contrast, other whiskeys blend a variety of malt and grain products from several distilleries.

The Tyrconnell, an authentic product of Ireland, is from Ireland's only independent, Irish-owned distillery, Coolery Distillery, Plc., in Riverstown, Dundalk, and Andrew A. Watt & Co., of County Louth.

The whiskey is full-bodied with a fresh, malty bouquet; smooth, sweet taste and a delicate, dry finish.

The brand is named for "The Tyrconnell," a chestnut colt that raced to victory at 100-1 odds to win the prestigious Queen Victoria Plate in the 1876 Irish National Produce Stakes. So impressed was the owner, that he named his flagship brand of Irish whiskey after his beloved horse.

The Tyrconnell Single Malt Irish Whiskey is available in 750 ml and 50 ml bottles.

A Bit Of The Others

Ballygeary

Launched in 1996 and available mainly in the United Kingdom. It is distilled at Cooley and blended by Invergordon, a Scottish distiller.

Buena Vista

The only blended Irish whiskey supplied on an exclusive basis by Irish distillers for the famous Buena Vista Cafe at Fisherman's Wharf in San Francisco, California. Used mainly for Irish Coffee and sold only at the Buena Vista Cafe.

Dunphy's

Available in the U.S. until 1988, but still available in the Irish Republic.

O'hara

An Irish blend for the supermarket chain "Intermarche" in France.

Old Dublin

Available in retail stores throughout the United Kingdom.

The Rest of the Best

Celtic Crossing

Celtic Crossing, a premium Irish Spirit liqueur new in the United States, came about as the result of a unique combination of heritage and creativity.

The delicate tasting liqueur is a blend of malt whiskeys, aged in oak barrels, with specially selected cognac from France. It is created in Ireland by the Gaelic Heritage Corporation, Limited, the product development and marketing arm of the Terra Group, an Independent Irish Company specializing in responding to niche opportunities in the world of international spirits.

Labels on the distinctive Celtic Crossing bottle and packaging refer to "150 years of Irish Heritage," the number of years since the Great Irish Famine. A special product enclosure brochure ends with this toast. "To remember those who left Irish shores never again to see their homeland and to celebrate the heritage and achievements of Irish people around the world. Slante."

Three different bottlings are being offered. One is a signed and limited edition bottling ($80 suggested retail) in a ceramic crock based on the original three-legged skillet pot used in many Irish homesteads in famine times. It is packaged in a rope-handled box resembling a ship's lantern with the luxury crock positioned in a three-dimensional window. The standard bottling (750ml/expected to retail under $20) is a 6"x75"x2" bottle with six individual label facings visible through the honey colored liqueur. A trade miniature (50ml) is also produced.

Cork Dry Gin

Cork Dry Gin is a gin of distinctive character and great purity. On a base of the finest triple distilled grain spirit is laid down a complex blend of juniper, citrus fruit and botanical flavours. On tasting, one is aware of these notes, but also of a background, almost subliminal dry slightly burnt flavour that is not found in other gins: this is the Watercourse* note. CDC Gin's unique ingredient that makes it that little bit different and very interesting.

Taste: Juniper with fruity citrus elements—orange peel noticeably. Also a vaguely medicinal undertone, "burnt coffee." Very clean and well balanced.

*Watercourse - a dry taste that is the trademark of Cork's historic Watercourse Distillery. No other gin has it. Cork Dry Gin has 90% of the Irish gin market.

Irish Mist
The Story Behind the
Legendary Liqueur

A legend, it is said, is a story popularly regarded as historical. A story passed down from generation to generation. A story that has survived time. So it is with Irish Mist® liqueur, for it is time that has made Irish Mist truly legendary. Born over 1200 years ago, Irish Mist has a heritage that parallels the heritage of Ireland itself. Here in this ancient land of rich, lush, green countrysides dotted with fabled castles and elegant estates, a most unique recipe was created. It was for heather wine, the very essence of what is today, Irish Mist. At the heart of that drink, savoured by the chieftains and nobles of Ireland's ancient clans, was a spirit touched with overtones of honey, herbs and spices.

But when the clans left their beloved country for wars on the European Continent, the recipe went with them. Regrettably, it was soon to be lost. Yet later, after its long, lamented absence, Ireland's heather wine was rediscovered for all time. The Williams', a renowned Irish distilling family desirous of rediscovering the ancient drink of their land for their distillery in Tullamore, met a traveler from Europe.

He arrived, quite fortuitously, with the long lost recipe that the distiller acquired and transformed into what is now the famous Irish Mist liqueur. Inherent in this transformation was a devotion to the authenticity and originality of Ireland's legendary liqueur. First there was the melange of distinctive ingredients to consider. Not one, but four great distilled spirits that form the liqueur's heart. Each spirit has its own character bred by its grains of origin, the inherent qualities of its wooden casks, even the time and geography of its maturation. Indeed, each spirit is also the result of distilling traditions with centuries of heritage. Once the spirits have mellowed and matured, a time-honoured blending mastery brings them together, and they are married. The marriage then leads to a resting period during which the four spirits become one. After a perfect balance is achieved, the blend is ready to be co-mingled with exquisite honeys and herbs. From the heather and clover that cover Ireland's landscape, the finest honey is naturally produced for Irish Mist.

Finally, as many as a dozen different herbs, exotic and delicately aromatic, are gathered from far and wide to join in and complete the marriage that has become legendary. The ultimate achievement is the taste of Irish Mist, a taste as luxurious as the package in which the liqueur is presented. In tribute to Irish Mist's ancient heritage and Irish traditions, there's the elegant decanter-style bottle. Its jewel-like facets sparkle with a clarity reminiscent of Ireland's prestigious Waterford® crystal, after which it was designed.

A classic, the bottle is enhanced by the sumptuousness of the Irish Mist label, a design inspired by the precious 8th Century Tara Brooch, one of the finest works of Ireland's Golden Age. Equally treasured chalices as well as other rare brooches, shields and regalia that adorned the royalty of the ancient clans provided further inspiration. Indeed, it is fitting that the treasures of Ireland embellish this classic liqueur.

Yet, as treasured and as exceptional as Irish Mist is, it is a liqueur for all occasions. Be it an elaborate celebration, a special night out, a moment for relaxed reflection, a sharing between two people, a thoughtful gift, or a friendly get-together, spontaneous and informal, Irish Mist is most welcome. After all, who among us can deny a desire for a beautiful sense of luxury? Let this liqueur flow into a glass and one's eye is captured by the rich, warm, golden tones, by the promise of something superb to come. Raise the glass to the nose and become immediately enchanted by the bouquet, delicate, elusive and so inviting.

Sip, and at once Irish Mist gloriously fulfills its promise, lives up to its legend, with all the subtle riches it alone possesses. Indeed, the only after-dinner choice worthy of consideration is between the classic Irish Mist neat, the inimitable Irish Mist with ice, or the harmonious Irish Mist and soda. Regardless of choice, one savors the taste time has made legendary, the taste of Irish Mist. Experience it. And experience the world's most luxurious liqueur.

The history of Meade

Meade is much more than an extraordinary, legendary drink with strong attachments to Ireland. In fact Meade can be traced back many centuries before Christ. Up to the middle ages, Meade was made from fermented honey and water by secretive monks. It was the chief drink of the Irish and was often referred to in Gaelic poetry. Its influence was so great that the halls of Tara, where the High Kings of Ireland ruled, was called the House of the Mead Circle. Meade's fame as a refreshing drink spread quickly and soon a medieval banquet was not complete without it.

Even the church recognized the value of Meade. Legend has it that St. Findian lived for six days a week on bread and water but on Sundays ate salmon and drank a full cup of Meade. In addition, St. Bridget performed a miracle when Meade could not be located for the King of Leinster—she blessed an empty vessel which miraculously became filled with Meade.

Soon Meade became very popular at weddings, where the

bride and groom were toasted with the honey-based drink. On numerous occasions the groom, laced with generous amounts of Meade, was carried by his friends to the bedside of his bride. If nine months later a bouncing baby boy appeared, credit was given to the Meade and its maker.

The monks' secret method of making Meade was lost during the tumultuous years of the middle ages. It wasn't until modern times that it reappeared. Today, Meade is once again being produced by the Irish at Bunratty Meade & Liqueur Co. Ltd., Bunratty, County Clare, Ireland. The result is a drink "fit for a king."

The Perfect Finale
To Wedding Receptions
how Meade Became
Wedded to Marriages

Have you ever attended a wedding reception where there seemed to be quite a bit of awkwardness and confusion at the end? What seems to happen quite often is that every aspect of the wedding and reception is carefully planned, according to custom and family tradition—except for the ending.

So the bride and groom usually go quietly off to change their clothes and slip away.

This certainly is not a new dilemma. As it happens, there's an ancient solution to the problem. How ancient? As far back as the Irish Middle Ages. The Irish had a tasteful answer to ending marriage ceremonies and celebrations: a toast with Meade.

The ancient Irish drink of Meade is once again bringing special meaning to weddings, and providing an excellent way to end them. After being lost for 500 years, the recipe for Meade has been rediscovered. So it is once again available to properly send a bride and groom off with a final toast and special poem.

Today, many Irish weddings are being ended with style and substance, because the full meaning of Meade is once again understood. And the tradition is spreading as it did centuries ago.

Ever since the fame of the Irish monks' brew spread throughout Medieval Ireland, it was believed that Meade was essential for sending off the bride and groom after the wedding. Meade was used both as a final toast and as a proper beginning to the marriage. The bride and groom were provided with enough

Meade, and special goblets, so that they could toast each other for one full moon — hence the term "Honeymoon."

This delicate yet potent drink was not only considered the best way to start a new marriage, it was also believed to enhance such valued qualities as fertility and virility.

The return of Meade has revived the unifying tradition of a formal, final wedding toast to the bride and groom. It provides a focused finale to the reception and also revives the full meaning of "Honeymoon."

Bunratty, the Irish distillers of Meade today, have created a special "Honeymoon Gift," which contains a potpourri, a gift sachet for the bride, a bottle of Meade, two glass goblets and the special poem.

Bunratty Meade

Bunratty Meade is produced to the highest standards of quality and is based on a recipe that was a jealously guarded secret for over a thousand years!

Bunratty Winery, located in County Clare, Ireland was originally an old coach house set in the shadow of the now famous 15th century Bunratty Castle.

Coachmen on their way to the West of Ireland would stop here and stable their horses for the night before continuing on their journey.

In 1979, the Coach House was restored to house the original Mead Winery and regularly receives visitors from throughout the world.

Mead was originally believed to have the powers of virility and fertility.

In fact, it soon became the custom for the bride and groom to drink this honey-based drink for one full moon after their wedding, and so the word "Honeymoon" was coined.

In Ireland today, it is still a tradition to toast the bride and groom with a glass of Meade.

The distinctive flavor of Bunratty Meade is the result of taking the world's finest honey and carefully blending it together with selected herbs and wine.

In your own home, this superlative drink may be enjoyed both lightly chilled as an aperitif, or at room temperature as a table wine.

Potcheen

The Original Irish Spirit For The Rest of The World to Savour

The illegal Irish drink is surrounded by myth, but one man has broken through the red tape.

It was truly a spiritual thing that the Irish did long ago when they trapped the pure and magical of nature to create from sunshine and rain, in the mountains and valleys, the original treasured spirit "Potcheen" of the Celtic Isle of Saints and Scholars.

Over many centuries, the manufacture of Potcheen (so called because it was distilled in pot stills in remote areas throughout Ireland) has been praised in song and story.

Distilling poitin—or potcheen if you like—has been illegal in Ireland since the Crown imposed a levy on spirits in 1661. Until now that is. For in the pleasant village of Bunratty in County Clare under the shadow of its historic castle, Oliver Dillon is making the stuff with the full legal sanction of the Irish Revenue Commissioners, provided he doesn't sell it in his own country.

Oliver Dillon is the Managing Director of the Bunratty Mead and Liqueur Company which has been producing mead for the past ten plus years.

For some years now Oliver Dillon has cherished the idea of making poitin and trying to win back its ancient good name presently tarnished by tales of stills in pig sties and on mountain tops producing spirits from potatoes and beet. He told me: "Poitin should only be made from the best of malt, barley, yeast, sugar and water."

So his next step was to gain official approval. Years ago, he approached the commissioners, the Republic's equivalent of the Customs and Excise. Their first reaction was to say that they were not impressed. But Oliver Dillon persisted and, after two years, he received permission. Poitin, which simply means "little pot," is the name Dillon prefers as it is the Gaelic version. Potcheen is the anglicised one.

Hackler

Poitín Irish Spirit

United Distillers, the spirits company of Guinness PLC, launched Hackler Irish Poitín on March 17, 1997. The product, which is distilled under license at Cooley Distillery near Dundalk, Co Louth, is a pure, high quality Irish alcohol. It has been developed by United Distillers to capture a significant share of the global young adult market for mixable white spirits.

Hackler is a refined, smooth—and legal—version of the infamous Poitín, illegally distilled in Ireland for over 300 years. Made from pure Irish water and grain, Hackler has a unique flavor and character. Its production has been approved by the Irish Revenue Commissioners.

Hackler Poitín is based on an old Irish poitín recipe and relies on distillation techniques that protect its purity and smoothness of character. Its single source of production and United Distillers' distilling skills and quality controls ensure the purity and consistency of the product.

The Hackler bottle is a contemporary, attractive design. The bottle carries the story of the "Hackler from Grousehall," explaining the source of the name Hackler, a Master Weaver and Craftsman.

"The Hackler of Grousehall was a distiller of highest quality illicit poitín in 19th century Ireland. The Master Craftsman would doubtless be pleased that after over so many years, this pure and smooth tasting Hackler Poitín is now legally available. Hackler now brings the spirit of Irish welcome and fun to people all around the world."

Hackler should have distribution in the U.K., U.S.A. and Australia in the very near future. Hackler will be marketed worldwide as the spirit which embodies Irish warmth, sociability, and fun. It can be drunk neat or tastes great with any mixer.

Irish Creams

Ashbourne Irish Cream

Imported by Marie Brizard Wines & Spirits, USA

Ashbourne Irish Cream Liqueur is a quality Irish Cream liqueur which is produced in Waterford Ireland for the international wine & spirits company, Marie Brizard.

The cream comes from one of the largest dairies in Ireland. This dairy is famous for its cream's quality and consistency. The marriage of this superb cream with Irish spirits is completed in an ultra-modern plant near the village of Ashbourne, in Waterford. Both facilities are internationally recognized for their quality and process controls.

Baileys Original Irish Cream Liqueur

The success of Baileys Original Irish Cream Liqueur is more than just the luck of the Irish. It is the creation of a mixture with the richness of cream, the tastes of vanilla, chocolate and other natural flavorings, and the spirit of fine Irish Whiskey.

Baileys is made from fresh dairy cream (not more than two hours old), Irish Whiskey, and natural flavorings. The mixture is then homogenized to ensure uniformity in every bottle, pasteurized to preserve freshness, and then cooled and bottled. The Irish Whiskey acts as a preservative of the cream, which is why Baileys does not have to be refrigerated, though it should be stored between 40 - 80 degrees Fahrenheit.

Baileys was introduced to the U.S. in 1979 after five years of painstaking research in dairy product technology. It is the first liqueur to successfully create a blend of real cream and spirits that is shelf-stable. Baileys has spawned a slew of imitators, but none of them have succeeded in capturing America's imagination — and taste buds — as has Baileys Original Irish Cream Liqueur.

Baileys St. Patrik's Day 1998 Irish Cream Liqueur

Most people consume Baileys straight up or on-the-rocks, though it is increasingly being used for a variety of mixed drinks. In winter it is often mixed with coffee or hot chocolate. Summer time consumption is moving to Baileys being blended with cream and crushed ice. Also, it is being blended with a scoop of ice cream into a cool thick malt. The forthcoming recipes show the surprising versatility of Baileys.

Baileys® Original Irish Cream Liqueur launched a Commemorative 200 ml bottle specially designed for St. Patrick's Day 1998. It is the first time Baileys has celebrated the Irish holiday with a special package.

The St. Patrick's Day limited-edition features a distinctive green shrink-wrapped bottle with lucky shamrocks. The special St. Patrick's Day 200 ml bottle will retain the same bottle shape as the core Baileys packaging. The inspiration for the bottle shape is the style of the old Irish whiskey crock, the traditional jug used for storing Irish whiskey.

Carolans Irish Cream

Carolans Irish Cream was developed in 1978 and launched in the United Kingdom in July 1979. Since the launch of Carolans, the brand has grown at a phenomenal rate to be the firmly established world's Number 2 Cream Liqueur, marketed in over 70 countries worldwide with sales of over 500,000 cases.

Carolans Irish Cream is named after the celebrated 17th century harpist, Turlough O'Carolan. Blind from an early age, he became one of the greatest and most well-known traveling harpists in Ireland. His tunes were distinctive and many of his lyrics reflected his lively and cheerful character. Carolans Irish Cream embodies the convivial spirit of its namesake. However, Turlough O'Carolan is not to be used for promoting the brand.

Carolans Irish Cream is a unique tasting, high quality cream liqueur. The fact that cream liqueurs originated in Ireland is no coincidence, for Ireland has a great tradition in producing fine quality dairy products and distilling spirits.

It is the marrying of these two traditions and Irish expertise that lies behind the success story of Carolans. Carolans combines aged Irish spirits and rich double cream. It derives its superior taste from the subtle blending of flavors, principally honey. It is the touch of honey that gives Carolans its distinctively subtle flavor and differentiates it from other Irish Creams.

This ingredient is very appropriate for a drink produced in Clonmel. The word Clonmel is derived from the Gaelic "Cluain Meala" which means Vale of Honey.

Clonmel, in County Tipperary, is also set in Ireland's famed "Golden Vale" probably the best natural dairyland in the world. Only the best suppliers are considered since the cream is such a vital component, making up over a third of the product. It is this uncompromising quality and use of the finest cream that gives Carolans such a smooth consistency.

Basically, there are four stages that go into the production of Carolans combining traditional expertise with modern, highly sophisticated technology.

1st Stage

Neutral spirit and Irish whiskey are carefully blended together in a vat at the plant to prepare the alcohol base for Carolans. Skill and experience play an important role in determining the perfect balance of spirits that are to be mixed with the cream. In addition, the alcohol base is closely monitored in the quality control laboratories to ensure exacting standards are met. When the right blend is achieved, it is mixed with the cream at a nearby dairy.

2nd Stage

Cream, water, and stabilizers are mixed together at high temperatures in large stainless steel tanks at the dairy. Stabilizers are essential to make sure that the product does not curdle. To get the mixture just right is a very delicate process indeed and is very tightly controlled using modern, sophisticated equipment.

3rd Stage

After an appropriate period, the cream mixture is fed through stainless steel piping to a homogenizer. During this process, the spirits, honey and flavors are fed into the mixture. The homogenization process ensures that the cream does not separate and binds all the ingredients together.

The technology which binds the cream and spirit in Carolans is unique and highly specialized ensuring long life and a full, fresh taste.

4th Stage

Following homogenization the mixture is cooled and bottled at the plant. Prior to bottling, samples are taken from every batch of Carolans for analysis and quality control. This close attention to quality ensures that the highest standards are maintained and only the best product is bottled.

The bottling hall at Clonmel was extended in 1988 in response to the continuing success of Carolans. We now have one of the most modern, efficient bottling plants which will contribute to Carolans future growth.

The secret behind the product's stability lies in the homogenization process. This breaks up the fat content into tiny molecules which remain suspended in the liquid and bound to the other ingredients; thus the cream will not separate from the liquid.

The technological advantage in the manufacturing process gives Carolans the best stability and the longest shelf life of all Irish cream liqueurs. On average Carolans will last in excess of 2 years unopened and one year opened, although it is best drunk within 6 months of being opened. Whilst not essential, it is recommended that the bottle be refrigerated once opened to keep it at its best.

Carolans is perishable and must be treated in the same way as fine wine.

Carolans stock must always be rotated on a first in, first out basis.

Carolans stock should be stored in a cool, dry place between 5 - 27 degrees Celsius (40 - 80 degrees Fahrenheit).

The above cannot be over-stressed. Good rotation ensures that product is always fresh and, while Carolans is the most "heat resistant" Irish cream liqueur on the market, exposure to excessively hot conditions will affect the subtle flavor characteristics of the product.

Devonshire
Royal Cream Liqueur

Devonshire Royal Cream Liqueur - the measure of perfection.

Few companies have successfully developed products from "the grape to the grain" but that's what Henry Devonshire & Co. Ltd., Ireland's independent wine and spirit producer, has achieved in truly remarkable fashion with Devonshire Royal Cream Liqueur.

This flagship brand encompasses four national heritages and weaves them magically together into a uniquely smooth blend of Scotch Whisky, French Brandy, and fresh Irish Cream from a traditional English recipe.

Devonshire Royal Peaches & Cream Liqueur - The subtle flavors of luscious sun-drenched peaches, the finest French Brandy, and fresh Irish Cream are blended together to form the perfect partnership.

O'Mara's Irish Country Cream

The Irish Cream category is vibrant, active and profitable, and it's expected to continue to grow over the next five years and expand on its popularity.

O'Mara's Irish Country Cream is an authentic product of Ireland and is the first Irish Cream to incorporate fine wine in its unique blending process. The wine base opens up additional retail distribution opportunities and provides a distinctly smooth flavor without a hint of harsh aftertaste.

It is hand-crafted in the heart of Ireland's dairy region by Pat O'Mara & Co. of Abbeyleix, Ireland, an independent Irish-owned liqueur company. The freshest, sweetest cream in all of Ireland is supplied for O'Mara's from a little dairy down the road.

O'Mara's Irish Country Cream has a unique bottle shape with a distinguishing magenta ribbon necker and wax-like medallion pressed with the O'Mara family crest.

O'Mara's Irish Country Cream is available in 750 ml bottles.

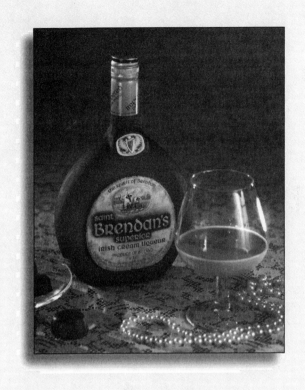

Saint Brendan's Superior
Irish Cream Liqueur

Saint Brendan's Superior is produced in the North West of Ireland — an area renowned for the quality of its dairies and distilleries. Nestled in the lush valley of Lough Foyle, the dairy selects only the finest ingredients to give Saint Brendan's Superior its distinctive creamy texture.

Using a complex, but natural process, local dairy cream is skillfully blended with an aged Irish Whiskey to produce this irresistible blend. Saint Brendan's Superior is free of artificial additives and is made with only natural ingredients.

Beamish

Quality and tradition run deep at Beamish. The business was founded on January 13, 1792 as The Cork Porter Brewery — a partnership among merchants William Beamish, William Crawford and two associates. The characteristically rich, nutty-tasting Beamish Stout is brewed today with a pedigree yeast that goes back almost 200 years. Strict control of the all-natural ingredients, including exceptionally soft water from the outskirts of Cork City, gives Beamish the unique flavor and character that has made it the number two selling stout brand in Ireland. Even the company's original 17th-Century building in Cranmer's Lane today still forms part of the Beamish & Crawford brewery, although the firm has adopted thoroughly modern brewing technology to assure an optimal product.

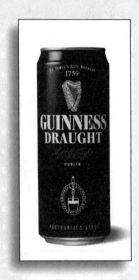

Guinness

The brand Guinness is the best-selling stout in the United States and around the world. Brewed at Dublin's St. James's Gate Brewery, Draught Guinness is sought after by beer drinkers who appreciate its rich black color, smooth creamy head and complex, well-balanced flavors.

Guinness has a fabled past and is proudly recognized as the original "Stout." In 1759, 34-year-old Arthur Guinness took over a small brewery on the outskirts of Dublin. After signing a 9,000-year lease at an annual rent of 45 pounds, Guinness started brewing ales and a relatively new beer called porter, so named because its characteristically dark color and rich flavor were popular with the porters of London's Covent Garden. Guinness' porter was so flavorful, yet smooth, that it set the standard for other brewers. By the 1820s, the adjective "stout" had been added to describe Guinness. Since that time, many brands have tried but have failed to duplicate the special appeal of Guinness. Today, Guinness is a globally recognized symbol of the Emerald Isle and, at home, is a traditional element of the Irish culture.

Draught Guinness starts with crystal clear water from Ireland's Wicklow Mountains, which contains the perfect balance of minerals for brewing a fine stout. High-quality domestic Irish barley is malted and mashed, then mixed with hand-picked hops, dark-roasted barley and a special strain of the original yeast used by Arthur Guinness to create the immediately recognizable deep black color, rich creamy head and enticing flavor that is Draught Guinness.

It is said that Draught Guinness is "first drunk with the eyes." To serve the perfect pint, the 50-liter (13.2-gallon) kegs of Guinness should be dispensed by a gas mixture of 75% nitrogen and 25% carbon dioxide at pressure between 30-40 pounds per square inch to produce the famous rich creamy head. Dispensed through the unique Guinness faucet, Draught Guinness is ideally served at between 42-48 degrees Fahrenheit.

Draught Guinness is an experience for all of the senses. It starts with the visual appeal of a perfectly built pint of Guinness, with its majestic thick head and mysteriously dark color. The aroma of a Guinness offers hints of the brew's complexity and balance. And the taste of Guinness delivers on the promise of a beer that is known and respected world-wide. The taste of Guinness is a rich mix of roasted barley, a slightly caramel flavor that is balanced by perfectly selected hops to create a drink that is at once both dry and refreshing. The aroma and rich creamy head of Guinness is best enjoyed in the classic tulip-shaped pint glass. Guinness is a great accompaniment to a wide range of fine foods. For example, try Guinness with oysters and shellfish or roasted meats and wild game.

While the Guinness brand is more than two centuries old, the popularity of Draught Guinness continues to increase. During the last 10 years this explosive growth has averaged 17.1% a year. In the last three years Draught Guinness has been growing at an astounding 25% annually.

Guinness is perhaps the world's most literary beer. George Bernard Shaw, Sean O'Casey, Brian O'Nalan, James Joyce and Graham Greene frequently mention the famous Irish stout in their works. "Ask them haven't they got a Guinness. I'd just fancy a Guinness." — Graham Greene's Stamboul Train.

Draught Guinness has just 10 calories per fluid ounce. That is less than most domestic lagers and about the same as skim milk. Draught Guinness has approximately 4% alcohol by volume.

Pub Draught Guinness

A pint of Draught Guinness is one of the most sought after beers on earth. In fact, Guinness is the best-selling stout in the United States and around the world. With the revolutionary Pub

Draught Guinness can, beer drinkers can enjoy the rich black color, smooth creamy head and complex, well-balanced flavors of Guinness—even if they cannot get to their local pub. The revolutionary Pub Draught Guinness can was invented by Guinness to simulate the draught experience and has won the brewery international awards, as well as the praise of thirsty customers.

Pub Draught Guinness starts with crystal clear water from Ireland's Wicklow Mountains, which contain the perfect balance of minerals for brewing a fine stout. High-quality domestic Irish barley is malted and mashed, then mixed with hand-picked hops, dark-roasted barley and a special strain of the original yeast used by Arthur Guinness to create the immediately recognizable deep black color, rich creamy head and enticing flavor unique to Guinness.

The innovative patented Pub Draught Guinness can replicates the famous special gas mixture that results in the perfect pint of stout. It is said that Guinness is "first drunk with the eyes," and the Pub Draught Guinness can delivers a perfect pint every time. Pub Draught Guinness is brewed and packaged in the patented can to capture the experience of a freshly pulled pint. It starts when the tab is pulled and the nitrogen is released and mixes with carbon dioxide. Guinness is ideally served at between 42-48 degrees Fahrenheit.

The visual appeal of a pint of Guinness, with its majestic thick head and mysteriously dark color, is the first indication that this is a special beer. The aroma of a Guinness offers hints of the brew's complexity and balance. And the taste of Pub Draught Guinness delivers on the promise of a beer that is known and respected worldwide. The taste of Guinness is a rich mix of roasted barley, a slightly caramel flavor that is balanced by perfectly selected hops to create a drink that is at once both dry and refreshing. The aroma and rich creamy head of Guinness is best enjoyed in the classic tulip-shaped pint glass. Guinness is excellent with oysters and shellfish. Try Pub Draught Guinness at a backyard barbecue; it makes a superb accompaniment to grilled meats.

Pub Draught Guinness was first sold in the United States in 1992.

The first packaged Guinness was sold in earthenware, handmade bottles. Later, Guinness was the first beer with "crown" sealed caps that are still used today.

While Guinness is brewed in 42 countries around the globe, all Guinness sold in the United States is brewed at the original St. James Gate Brewery in Dublin.

Harp Lager

The brand, Harp Lager, is a classic European-style lager brewed by the master brewers at Harp Brewery, Dundalk, County Louth, Ireland. A rich and flavorful lager, Harp is recognized for its crisp, clean taste. Harp is a favorite of lager fans across Europe and throughout the United States.

Harp Lager traces its roots deep in the Guinness brewing tradition. As consumption of lager in Ireland and Britain increased dramatically, Arthur Guinness Son & Company saw the potential for a high-quality lager. To meet this demand, they transformed the Great Northern Brewery in Dundalk, a stout and ale brewery, into the Harp Lager Brewery. The master brewers of Guinness created a rich golden lager, brewed in the continental style, and named it Harp, after the symbol on the Guinness trademark and of the Irish nation. Harp is exported to more than 30 countries around the world. Harp's distinctive, refreshing taste has earned seven gold medals against international competition in Belgium's famous Monde Selection beer tastings.

Water from the beautiful Cooley Mountains is combined with the finest ingredients available in Europe. Barley malt from Ireland, Saaz and Hallertau hops from Germany and the Czech Republic, and a prized lager yeast from Bavaria give Harp Lager its distinctive, refreshing taste. Harp Lager has 5% alcohol by volume.

Harp Lager is available on draught in 13.2 gallon kegs, and 12-ounce bottles packed four six packs to a case. To guarantee proper dispensing, draught Harp should be dispensed with carbon dioxide or a carbon dioxide and nitrogen blend, through clean lines and in beer-clean glassware. Like all lager, Harp should be stored and served at 40-42 degrees Fahrenheit.

Harp Lager is a sparkling golden lager with a pleasing aroma. Harp is a classic European-style lager, instantly refreshing with a hoppiness that is balanced by wonderful malty tones. Harp is a rich, flavorful lager with true Irish ancestry. Harp has the versatility to accompany fine continental cuisine or more casual fare.

The traditional recipe for a Half and Half combines draught Guinness and Harp Lager.

In the United States, Harp Lager has grown steadily in popularity. Harp Lager is the number one selling Irish lager.

Murphy's Irish Amber

In 1854, James J. Murphy and three of his brothers, Francis J., William J., and Jerome, bought the premises of the former Cork Foundling Hospital. Over the following two years, the existing buildings were adapted, where appropriate, and other construction added to form Lady's Well Brewery which commenced operations in 1856 under the style of James J. Murphy & Co.

The Murphy brothers were members of a family that had, over the previous 60 years or so, established itself as one of the wealthiest and most successful in Cork city. The family had made the larger part of its fortune in tanning, tea-importing and distilling.

When Lady's Well brewery went into production, there were already three successful breweries in Cork: Beamish & Crawford, Lane & Co., and Sir John Arnott & Co. Many considered the Murphy brothers' new venture very foolhardy. A 19th century account writes:

"Yet, undeterred by all the obstacles that beset their path, undaunted by the influences against which they had to combat, the Messrs. Murphy put their shoulders to the wheel and soon came to be recognized as one of the principal brewing establishments in our city."

The new firm established a reputation for its products and trade grew steadily through the latter decades of that century. By the late 1880s, it was producing more stout and porter than any of its rivals in the city. It was also acquiring a tied estate that guaranteed an outlet for its produce. New buildings and equipment were added as demand for James J. Murphy & Co.'s products grew. In 1892, a newspaper remarked that the extensive brewery premises "give an instructive insight into the prosperity that has attended the firm from its inception." Another account from 1894 states:

"It is difficult to describe with accuracy and fullness premises which are being almost daily improved, both as to construction and contents, and which are being constantly increased in size and importance."

The company had agents in a number of cities in Britain at this time and they enjoyed success in promoting Murphy's XX Stout, which was beginning to displace porter in popular taste. Efforts were also being made across the Atlantic. A contemporary source writes:

"...in America, those of our exiled kith and kin in that country will be in a position to sip of the creamy stout brewed within sight and within sound of some of the most historic scenes of their boyhood's years."

In 1901, James J. Murphy & Co. took over the brewing firm of Sir John Arnott & Co. and, in the process, almost doubled the size of its estate of tied houses to nearly 200. The early years of the 10th century were not unkind to the firm. It survived the First World War relatively well but, in the following years the fortunes of James J. Murphy & Co. began to falter.

The Irish War of Independence and the Civil War that followed caused severe difficulties between 1920 and 1923. The following 40 years or so never saw the brewery regain the growth and success of its first 50 years. There was no real reinvestment and while the shareholders received their dividends, whether from trading profits or reserves, things drifted on from year to year.

In the 1950s and more especially in the 1960s, business was becoming very competitive and tastes and lifestyles were changing. James J. Murphy & Co. did not at first react to these changes, but in the mid-1960s, it formed a joint venture with the Watney-Mann brewing concern of the U.K. to produce and market Red Barrel ale. New facilities were built and sales of Red

Barrel quickly grew. Set-up and distribution costs were very high, however, and placed a severe strain not only on the cash resources of James J. Murphy & Co., but also on the partnership with Watney-Mann. The partnership was dissolved in 1971 and the company was saved from liquidation by the state-owned business-rescue agency Taisci Stait (later Foir Teo).

In 1974, a large group of publicans formed the Licensed Vintners Co-Operative Society and bought 49% of James J. Murphy & Co. and Murphy's Brewery Ltd. was created. Two years later they bought the remaining 51% from Foir Teo. During the second half of the 1970s, the range of products offered expanded greatly. Publicans were offered a wide portfolio of wines, spirits, soft drinks, ales and lager in addition to stout. To fund expansion the tied houses, that for so long had largely sustained the brewery, were sold off. A new bottling plant was built.

In 1978, Murphy's Brewery Limited launched Heineken lager in Ireland. While a number of disasters struck the company around this time, the Heineken connection was eventually to ensure the survival of the brewery. The new bottling plant was not a success. Youngers Ale, which had also been recently launched, failed. Market and other conditions adversely affected the brewery. Over the following few years, the crisis deepened and, in July 1982, a receiver was appointed.

Following protracted negotiations, Heineken acquired the assets of Murphy's Brewery Ltd. in 1983 and Murphy Brewery Ireland Ltd. came into being. This ushered in the latest and probably most successful period in the 140 year history of Lady's Well Brewery.

Irish Cocktail Recipes

The Best
of all Irish Cocktails
for the first time in one Book

A.I
2/3 Cork Dry Gin
1/3 Grand Marnier
Dash Lemon Juice
Dash Grenadine
Lemon Twist
Shake with ice. Serve over ice with lemon twist.

ALASKA
3/4 Cork Dry Gin
1/4 Yellow Chartreuse
Shake with ice and serve.

A TINKER TALL
1 1/4 oz. Irish Mist
3 oz. Ginger Ale
3 oz. Club Soda
Lots of ice in a tall glass.

A-BOMB

1/2 oz. Baileys Original Irish Cream
1/2 oz. Kahlua
1/2 oz. Stolichnaya
1/4 oz. Tia Maria
Shaker can 1/2 ice. Put recipe into can. Shake and strain.

ABSOLUT QUAALUDE

1 oz. Baileys Original Irish Cream
1 oz. Frangelico
1 oz. Absolut
Shaker can 1/2 ice. Put recipe into shaker can. Stir and strain into sour glass filled with ice.

AFTER 8

1/2 oz. Baileys Original Irish Cream
1/2 oz. Kahlua
1/2 oz. Green Creme de Menthe
Shake. Serve straight up in shot glass.

ALMOND COW

1 1/2 oz. O'Mara's Irish Country Cream
1/2 oz. Lazzaroni Amaretto
2 oz. Half & Half
Shake together well; pour over ice.

AMBUSH

1 oz. Bushmills Irish Whiskey
1 oz. Amaretto
5 oz. Coffee
Serve hot in mug. Top with whipped cream if desired.

AUNT ROSE

1 1/4 oz. Irish Mist
2 oz. Cranberry Juice
2 oz. Orange Juice
Shake. Serve in tall glass with ice.

B ORIGINAL

The traditional way to enjoy Baileys is to serve a double measure in its own special glass at room temperatures. In warmer weather
many prefer it chilled before serving.

B-52

1 part Baileys Original Irish Cream
1 part Kahlua
1 part Triple Sec
Layer into a small snifter or large shot glass.

BAILEYS SHILLELAGH

1 part Baileys Original Irish Cream
1 part Romana Sambuca
A ShamRocket Shot!

BAILEYS & COFFEE
Pour 1 1/2 oz. Baileys Original Irish Cream into a cup of steaming coffee.

BAILEYS ALEXANDER
2 oz. Baileys Original Irish Cream
1 part Cognac
Shake well with ice and serve on the rocks or strain into cocktail glass.

BAILEYS ALMOND CREAM
2 parts Baileys Original Irish Cream
2 parts Light Cream
dash Pure Almond Extract
Combine all ingredients in shaker. Shake and pour over ice.

BAILEYS CHOCOLATE COVERED CHERRY
1/2 oz. Baileys Original Irish Cream
1/2 oz. Grenadine
1/2 oz. Kahlua
Layer grenadine
Kahlua
then Baileys. As a shot or on the rocks.

BAILEYS COCONUT FRAPPE
2 parts Baileys Original Irish Cream
1 part Malibu Rum
2 parts Milk
Shake or blend until frothy; pour over ice and garnish with toasted coconut.

BAILEYS CREAM DREAM

2 oz. Baileys Original Irish Cream
2 oz. Half & Half
4 oz. Ice Cubes
Blend for 30 seconds.

BAILEYS CUDDLER

1 1/2 oz. Baileys Original Irish Cream
1 1/2 oz. Di Saronno Amaretto
Combine ingredients for a truly spirited pleasure.

BAILEYS DUBLIN DOUBLE

1 part Baileys
1 part Di Saronno Amaretto
A ShamRocket Shot!

BAILEYS EGGNOG

1 oz. Baileys Original Irish Cream
1/2 oz. Irish Whiskey
1 medium Egg
2 cups Milk
Nutmeg
Mix with cracked ice in a shaker, strain and serve
in tall glasses. Sprinkle nutmeg.

BAILEYS FIZZ

2 oz. Baileys Original Irish cream
1 oz. Club Soda
Pour over crushed ice.

BAILEYS FLOAT

2 oz. Baileys Original Irish Cream
2 scoops Softened Ice Cream
Blend ingredients until frothy. Top with one more
scoop of ice cream.

BAILEYS FRENCH DREAM

1 1/2 oz. Baileys Original Irish Cream
1/2 oz. Raspberry Liqueur
2 oz. Half & Half
4 oz. Ice Cubes
Blend for 30 seconds.

BAILEYS GODET TRUFFLE

Equal parts:
Baileys Original Irish Cream
Godet
Serve on the rocks.

BAILEYS HOT MILK PUNCH

1 oz. Baileys Original Irish Cream
1/4 oz. Cognac
1 1/2 tsp. Sugar
3 parts Hot Milk
dash Freshly Ground Nutmeg
Combine Baileys and Cognac to dissolve sugar.
Add hot milk and stir. Sprinkle with nutmeg.

BAILEYS ICED CAPPUCCINO

Brew a pot of double-strength coffee and set aside to cool. In a blender combine:

1/2 cup Ice

2 oz. Baileys Original Irish Cream

5 oz. Double-strength Coffee

1 oz. Half & Half

2 tsp. Sugar

Blend for ten seconds and pour into a 10 oz. glass filled with ice. Top with a dollop of whipped cream and sprinkle of cinnamon if desired.

BAILEYS IRISH COFFEE

1 part Baileys Original Irish Cream

1/2 part Irish Whiskey

4 parts Freshly Brewed Coffee

1 Tbsp. Whipped Sweetened Cream

After brewing coffee combine with Baileys and whiskey. Top with cream.

BAILEYS ITALIAN DREAM

1 1/2 oz. Baileys Original Irish Cream

1/2 oz. DiSaronno Amaretto

2 oz. Half & Half

4 oz. Ice Cubes

Blend for 30 seconds and serve.

BAILEYS MINT KISS

2 parts Baileys Original Irish Cream
5 parts Coffee
1 part Rumple Minze Peppermint Schnapps
Top with fresh whipped cream.

BAILEYS MIST

2 oz. Baileys Original Irish Cream
Pour in a glass filled with crushed ice. Delicious!

BAILEYS O'

Equal parts:
Baileys Original Irish Cream
Stolichnaya Ohranj

BAILEYS ROMA

1 part Baileys Original Irish Cream
1 part Romana Sambuca
Pour over ice and serve.

BAILEYS RUM YUM

1 oz. Baileys Original Irish Cream
1 oz. Malibu Rum
1 oz. Cream or Milk
Blend with ice.

BAILEYS SLIPPERY ELF

1 part Baileys Original Irish Cream
1 part Smirnoff Vodka
Serve in a shot glass.

BAILEYS SUNSET

1 part Baileys Original Irish Cream
1 part Triple Sec
1 part Kahlua
Gently layer the Kahlua then the Baileys followed
by the Triple Sec. Garnish with orange for a triple
layer of delight.

BALLSBRIDGE BRACER

1 1/2 oz. Tullamore Dew
3/4 oz. Irish Mist
3 oz. Orange Juice
1 Egg White (for two drinks)
Mix all ingredients with cracked ice in a shaker or
blender. Strain into a chilled whiskey sour glass.

BALLYLICKEY BELT

1 1/2 oz. Jameson Irish Whiskey
1/2 tsp. Heather Honey or to taste
Club Soda
Lemon Peel
Muddle heather honey with a little water or club
soda until dissolved and pour in whiskey. Add
several ice cubes and fill with club soda. Twist
lemon peel over drink and drop into glass.

BANANA DREAM

2/10 Cork Dry Gin
1/10 Cointreau
2/10 Bols Creme de Bananes
2/10 Lemon Cordial
3/10 Fresh Pouring Cream
Lemon, Chocolate Flake
Shake.

BARNUMENTHE & BAILEYS

1 1/2 oz. Baileys Original Irish Cream
1/2 oz. White Creme de Menthe
In a rocks glass over cracked ice.

BERMUDIAN ROSE

2/5 Cork Dry Gin
1/5 Apricot Brandy
1/5 Grenadine
1/5 Lemon Juice
Shake with ice.

BLACK AND TAN

A 10 to 14 oz. glass
1 1/2 oz. Tullamore Dew
1 oz. Jamaica Dark Rum
1/2 oz. Lime Juice
1/2 oz. Orange Juice
1/2 tsp. Superfine Sugar
6-8 Ice Cubes
4 oz. Ginger Ale chilled
Combine Irish Whiskey, rum, lime and orange juice, sugar and 3 to 4 ice cubes in shaker and shake vigorously. Put remaining ice in glass. Strain mixture into glass and fill with ginger ale.

BLACK MANHATTAN

1 1/2 oz. Old Bushmills Black Bush Irish Whiskey
1/4 oz. Sweet Vermouth
Fill mixing glass with ice. Add Old Bushmills Black Bush Irish Whiskey and Sweet Vermouth. Stir; strain into a chilled martini glass or rocks glass filled with ice. Garnish with a cherry.

BLACK VELVET

1 part Guinness Stout
1 part Champagne
Layer the champagne over the Guinness in a champagne flute.

BLACKTHORN

1 oz. Jameson Irish Whiskey
1/4 oz. Dry Vermouth
1 dash Anisette
Stir well with cubed ice. Strain into cocktail glass
or serve on the rocks. Garnish with lemon twist.

BLACKTHORN #2

1 1/2 oz. Bushmills Irish Whiskey
1/2 oz. Noilly Prat Dry Vermouth
dash Anisette
Stir with ice. Serve in cocktail glass.

BLARNEY COCKTAIL

1 1/2 oz. Jameson Irish Whiskey
1 oz. Italian Vermouth
2 dashes Green Creme de Menthe
Shake well with ice. Strain into cocktail glass.
Serve with green cherry.

BLARNEY STONE COCKTAIL

2 oz. Kilbeggan Irish Whiskey
1/2 tsp. Pernod
1/2 tsp. Triple Sec
1/4 tsp. Grenadine
1 dash Angostura Bitters
Shake well with cracked ice and strain into 3 oz.
cocktail glass. Twist of orange peel and serve with
an olive.

BLOODY MOLLY

1 1/2 oz. Jameson Irish Whiskey
3 oz. Tomato Juice (seasoned to taste) or prepared
Bloody Mary Mix
dash Lemon Juice
Pour into tall glass over ice and stir
garnishing with celery heart.

BLOOMIN' APPLE

1 1/4 oz. Jameson Irish Whiskey
2 oz. Apple Juice
dash Cointreau
Pour into mixing glass. Method: ice, stir, decorate
with orange rind.

BLUE BLAZER

2 measures Tullamore Dew
1 measure Clear Honey
1/2 measure Lemon Juice
1-3 measures Water
Cinnamon Sticks (garnish)
Pour all ingredients into a pan and heat very gently until the honey has dissolved. Place a teaspoon into a short tumbler and pour drink carefully into the glass (the spoon prevents the glass from cracking).
Serve with cinnamon sticks.

BLUE FOR YOU
3/10 Cork Dry Gin
2/10 Blue Curacao
2/10 Bols Creme de Bananes
2/10 Cinzano (Dry)
2 Tsp. Cream
1/10 Pineapple Juice
Orange Peel, Green Cherry, Pineapple Leaves

BOILERMAKER
1 1/4 oz. Kilbeggan Irish Whiskey
10 oz. Beer
Serve whiskey in a shot glass with a glass of beer
on the side as a chaser.

BOW STREET SPECIAL
1 1/2 oz. Irish Whiskey
3/4 oz. Triple Sec
1 oz. Lemon Juice
Mix with cracked ice in a shaker or blender and
strain into a chilled cocktail glass.

BRAIN
3/4 shot Carolans Irish Cream
1/4 shot Peach Schnapps
Serve in a shot glass.

BRAIN HEMMORRHAGE
3/4 shot Carolans Irish Cream
1/4 shot Peach Schnapps
dash Grenadine
Serve in a shot glass.

BRAINSTORM

1 3/4 oz. Irish Whiskey
1/4 oz. Dry Vermouth
dash Benedictine
Stir all ingredients in a tumbler or jug then strain
into a cocktail glass. Decorate with a twist of
orange peel.

BRENDAN'S BULL DOG

3 oz. Saint Brendan's Superior Irish Cream
1 1/2 oz. Coffee Liqueur
splash Cola
Mix and serve over ice.

BRENDAN'S CHOCOLATE CHERRY

1 oz. Saint Brendan's Superior Irish Cream
1/2 oz. Coffee Liqueur
1/2 oz. Grenadine
Mix and serve over ice.

BRENDAN'S COFFEE ROYALE

1/2 oz. Saint Brendan's Superior Irish Cream
1/2 oz. Grand Marnier
1/2 oz. Coffee Liqueur
Fill with coffee. Top with whipped cream.

BRENDAN'S COOL FIZZ

3 oz. Saint Brendan's Superior Irish Cream
3 oz. Club Soda
Serve with crushed ice.

BRENDAN'S SMOOTHIE
1/2 oz. Saint Brendan's Superior Irish Cream
1/2 oz. Coffee Liqueur
1/2 oz. Vodka
1 oz. Milk or Cream

BRONX
1/2 Cork Dry Gin
1/6 Dry Vermouth
1/6 Sweet Vermouth
1/6 Fresh Orange Juice
Shake with ice.

BUCKING IRISH OR IRISH HIGHBALL
1 1/4 oz. Irish Whiskey
5 oz. Ginger Ale
Combine in ice cube-filled highball glass. Garnish
with lemon twist.

BUNGI JUMPER
1 1/4 oz. Irish Mist
4 oz. Orange Juice
1/2 oz. Cream
splash Amaretto
Mix all but Amaretto. Float Amaretto on top.

BUNRATTY PEG
1 1/2 oz. Tullamore Dew
3/4 oz. Irish Mist
Stir with ice and strain into a chilled cocktail glass
or with ice cubes in an old-fashioned glass.

BUSHMILLS COLLINS

1 oz. Bushmills Irish Whiskey
4 oz. Sweet & Sour Mix
1 oz. Club Soda
Shake Bushmills and sweet and sour. Top with club soda. Serve over ice.

BUSHMILLS FUZZY VALENCIA

1 1/2 oz. Bushmills Irish Whiskey
3/4 oz. Amaretto
5 oz. Orange Juice
Serve in tall glass over ice.

BUSHMILLS HOT IRISH TEA

1 1/2 oz. Bushmills Irish whiskey
4 oz. Hot Tea
In a mug stir well. Add cinnamon stick.

BUSHMILLS O'THENTIC IRISH KISS

1 1/2 oz. Bushmills Irish Whiskey
1 oz. Peach Schnapps
2 oz. Orange Juice
5 oz. Ginger Ale
Add ice and garnish with wedge of lime.

BUSHMILLS SUMMER SOUR

1 1/4 oz. Bushmills
2 oz. Orange Juice
2 oz. Sweet & Sour Mix
Shake; serve over rocks in collins glass.

BUSHMILLS SURPRISE

1 oz. Bushmills
1/2 oz. Triple Sec
2 oz. Lemon Juice
Shake well with ice and strain into cocktail glass.

BUSHMILLS TEA

1 1/2 oz. Bushmills Irish Whiskey
6 oz. Iced Tea
Serve in tall glass over ice. Garnish with lemon
twist.

BUSHMILLS TRIPLE TREAT

1 1/2 oz. Bushmills
3/4 oz. Amaretto
5 oz. Orange Juice
Serve in a tall glass over ice.

BUTTER FINGER

1/4 shot Irish Cream
1/4 shot Vodka
1/4 shot Butterscotch Schnapps
1/4 shot coffee-flavored liqueur (Kahlua)
Serve as a shot.

BUTTERY NIPPLE

1/3 shot Irish Cream
1/3 shot Vodka
1/3 shot Butterscotch Schnapps
Serve as a shot.

CAFFE BRENDAN'S

1 1/2 oz. Saint Brendan's Superior Irish Cream
1 1/2 oz. Coffee Liqueur
Shake with ice.

CAMERON'S KICK COCKTAIL

3/4 oz. Irish Whiskey
3/4 oz. Scotch Whisky
Juice of 1/4 Lemon
2 dashes Angostura Bitters
Shake well with cracked ice and strain into 3 oz.
cocktail glass.

CARIBBEAN CRUISE SHOOTER

2/3 shot Baileys Original Irish Cream
2/3 shot Kahlua Coffee Liqueur
2/3 shot Coco Ribe
Serve in pony/cordial glass. Shoot drink!

CAROLARETTO

1 part Carolans Irish Cream
1 part Amaretto
Shake or stir on the rocks.

CELTIC BULL

1 1/2 oz. Jameson Irish Whiskey
2 oz. Beef Consomme or Bouillon
2 oz. Tomato Juice
Several dashes Worcestershire Sauce
dash Tabasco Sauce
Freshly Ground Pepper
Mix all ingredients with cracked ice in a shaker or
blender. Pour into a chilled old-fashioned glass.

CEMENT MIXER
3/4 shot Irish Cream
1/4 shot Lime Juice
Pour directly into glass. Let stand for 30 seconds
and drink will coagulate. Serve in a shot glass.

CHIP SHOT
3/4 oz. Devonshire Irish Cream
3/4 oz. Tuaca
1 1/2 oz. Coffee
Serve on the rocks or in a shot glass.

CLARIDGE
1/3 Cork Dry Gin
1/3 Dry Vermouth
1/6 Cointreau
1/6 Apricot Brandy
Mix over ice.

COCKTAIL NA MARA (Cocktail of the Sea)
2 oz. Irish Whiskey
2 oz. Clam Juice
4 oz. Tomato Juice
1/2 oz. Lemon Juice
Several dashes Worcestershire Sauce
dash Tabasco Sauce
pinch White Pepper
Stir all ingredients well in a mixing glass with
cracked ice and pour into a chilled highball glass.

COCOLOU

1 part Carolans Irish Cream
1 part Creme de Cacao
Stir well on the rocks.

COFFEE ROYALE

1 part Saint Brendan's Superior Irish Cream
1 part Orange Liqueur/Grand Marnier, or Cointreau
1 part Coffee Liqueur
Fill with hot coffee and whipped cream.

COMMANDO FIX

A whiskey sour glass chilled
Crushed ice to fill whiskey sour glass
2 oz. Irish Whiskey
1/4 oz. Cointreau
1/2 oz. Lime Juice
1-2 dashes Raspberry Liqueur
Fill glass with ice. Add Irish Whiskey, Cointreau and
lime juice and stir slowly. Dot surface of drink with
raspberry liqueur.

CONNEMARA CLAMMER

2 oz. Irish Whiskey
2 oz. Clam Juice
3 oz. V-8 Juice
1 tsp. Lime Juice
Several dashes Worcestershire Sauce
1/2 tsp. Horseradish
Several pinches Freshly Ground Black or White Pepper
Mix all ingredients with cracked ice in a shaker or
blender. Strain into a chilled double old-fashioned glass.

COOL MIST
1 part Irish Mist
Tonic Water
Serve in a tall glass with crushed ice.

CORK COMFORT
1 1/2 oz. Jameson Irish Whiskey
3/4 oz. Sweet Vermouth
Several dashes Angostura Bitters
Several dashes Southern Comfort
Mix all ingredients with cracked ice in a shaker or
blender. Pour into a chilled old-fashioned glass.

COUNTY CLARE COOLER
3 oz. Bunratty Meade
7-Up
Ice
Lemon Slice
Serve over ice in tall glass.

COWCATCHER
1 part O'Mara's Irish Country Cream
1 part Sambuca Sarti
Mix together. Pour over ice and serve.

CREAM WHISKEY
1 part Carolans Irish Cream
2 part Rye Whiskey
Stir well on the rocks.

CREAMED SHERRY

2 parts Carolans Irish Cream
1 part Duff Gordon Cream Sherry
Stir well on the rocks.

CROCODILE BITE

1 1/4 oz. Jameson Irish Whiskey
2 oz. Orange Juice
1 oz. Grand Marnier
7-Up
Serve in a tall glass with ice. Garnish with a slice
of orange/lemon.

CUPID'S BOW

1/4 Cork Dry Gin
1/4 Forbidden Fruit Liqueur
1/4 Curacao
1/4 Passion Fruit Juice
Shake with ice.

DANCING LEPRECHAUN

1 1/2 oz. Jameson Irish Whiskey
1 1/2 oz. Lemon Juice
Club Soda
Ginger Ale
Combine the whiskey and the juice; shake with
ice. Strain and add ice. Fill the glass with equal
parts soda and ginger ale; stir gently. Touch it up
with a twist of lemon.

DERRY DELIGHT

2 oz. O'Mara's Irish Country Cream
2 oz. Half & Half
Shake together well; pour over ice cubes.

DERRY DELIGHT - WITH A KICK

1 1/2 oz. O'Mara's Irish Country Cream
1/2 oz. Copa De Oro Coffee Liqueur
1/2 oz. Burnett's Vodka
2 oz. Half & Half
Shake together well; pour over ice cubes.

DINGLE DRAM

1 1/2 oz. Tullamore Dew
1/2 oz. Irish Mist
Coffee Soda
dash Creme de Cacao
Whipped Cream
Pour Irish Whiskey and Irish Mist into a chilled highball glass along with several ice cubes. Fill with coffee soda. Stir gently. Add a float of Creme de Cacao. Top with dollop of whipped cream.

DIRTY GIRL SCOUT COOKIE

2/3 shot Carolans Irish Cream
1/3 shot Green Creme de Menthe
Serve as a shot.

DOUBLE IRISH COFFEE

1 part Saint Brendan's Superior Irish Cream
1 part Irish Whiskey
Fill with hot coffee and whipped cream.

DUBLIN HANDSHAKE

1/2 oz. Baileys Original Irish Cream
1/2 oz. Irish Whiskey
3/4 oz. Sloe Gin
Shake with crushed ice. Strain into cocktail glass.

ECLIPSE

1 1/2 oz. Old Bushmills Black Bush Irish
Whiskey
Seltzer
Fill a highball glass with ice. Add Old Bushmills
Black Bush Irish Whiskey. Stir. Top with seltzer.
Garnish with a slice of orange.

EMERALD ISLE

3/4 shot Tullamore Dew
3/4 shot Green Creme de Menthe
2 scoops Vanilla Ice Cream
Soda Water
Blend first 3 ingredients then add soda water. Stir
after adding soda water.

ERIE TOUR

1/3 Irish Mist
1/3 Carolans Irish Cream
1/3 Irish Whiskey
Serve over ice.

ERIN GO BURRR

3 oz. Carolans Irish Cream well chilled
Serve chilled Carolans straight up in a chilled
cocktail glass.

EXTRA NUTTY IRISHMAN

Equal Parts:
Irish Mist
Frangelico
Carolans Irish Cream
Shake. Top with whipped cream. Serve in a goblet
glass.

EYES R SMILIN

1 oz. Baileys Original Irish Cream
1 oz. Vodka
1/2 oz. Gin
1/2 oz. Triple Sec
Build over ice. Stir and serve.

FALLEN ANGEL

3/4 Cork Dry Gin
1/4 Fresh Lemon or Lime Juice
2 dashes White Creme de Menthe
1 dash Angostura Bitters
Shake with ice.

FIFTH AVENUE

1/2 oz. Baileys Original Irish Cream
1/2 oz. Apricot Brandy
1/2 oz. White Creme de Cacao
Shake with ice. Strain into cocktail glass.

FOUR LEAF CLOVER

1/4 oz. Bushmills
2 oz. Orange Juice
2 oz. Sweet & Sour Mix
splash Green Creme de Menthe
Shake first three ingredients and top with Creme
de Menthe.

FOUR-LEAF CLOVER

1 oz. Bushmills Irish Whiskey
2 oz. Orange Juice
2 oz. Sweet & Sour Mix
splash Green Creme de Menthe
Shake first three ingredients and strain into cocktail glass. Float green Creme de Menthe on top.

FOURTH DEGREE

1/3 Cork Dry Gin
1/3 Dry Vermouth
1/3 Sweet Vermouth
2 dashes Pernod
Mix with ice.

FRUITY IRISHMAN

2 parts Carolans Irish Cream
1 part Midori Melon Liqueur
Stir well on the rocks.

GEORGE BUSH

Crushed ice to fill glass to 3/4 level
1 1/2 oz. Old Bushmills Irish Whiskey
1 strip Lemon Peel
3-4 oz. Ginger Ale chilled
Fill glass with crushed ice to 3/4 level. Add Irish
Whiskey. Twist lemon peel over drink to release oil
and drop it in. Top with ginger ale.

GIMLET

2/3 Cork Dry Gin
1/3 Lime Juice Cordial
Mix with ice.

GIN FIZZ

Measure Cork Dry Gin
Juice of 1 Lemon
Tsp. of Castor Sugar
Shake and strain. Top with soda water.

GINGER MIST

1 part Irish Mist
3 parts Ginger Ale
Serve in a tall glass with wedge of lime.

GINOLANS

2 parts Carolans Irish Cream
1 part Gordon's Gin
Stir well and serve on the rocks.

GLENBEIGH FIZZ

1 1/2 oz. Tullamore Dew
1 oz. Medium Sherry
1/2 oz. Creme de Noyaux
1/2 oz. Lemon Juice
Club Soda
Pour all ingredients except club soda with several
ice cubes in a chilled highball glass and stir. Fill
with club soda.

GRAFTON STREET SOUR

1 1/2 oz. Irish Whiskey
1/2 oz. Triple Sec
1 oz. Lime Juice
1/4 oz. Raspberry Liqueur
Mix all ingredients except raspberry liqueur with
cracked ice in a shaker or blender and strain into
a chilled cocktail glass. Top with raspberry
liqueur.

GREEN DEVIL

A whiskey sour glass chilled
2 oz. Tullamore Dew
2 oz. Clam Juice
Shake with ice and serve.

GRIT COCKTAIL
1/2 jigger Tullamore Dew
1/2 jigger Italian Vermouth
Shake then strain into a cocktail glass.

GUARDS
2/3 Cork Dry Gin
1/3 Sweet Vermouth
3 dashes Orange Curacao
Mix with ice.

GYPSY'S KISS
1 part Irish Mist
1 part Orange Juice
1 part Lemon Juice or Sour Mix
Serve with a dash of grenadine (optional) in a
cocktail glass.

HAVANA
1/4 Cork Dry Gin
1/2 Apricot Brandy
1/4 Swedish Punch
Dash Lemon Juice
Shake with ice and serve over ice.

HAWAIIAN
1/2 Cork Dry Gin
1/2 Orange Juice
Dash Orange Curacao
Shake with ice and serve over ice.

HAWAIIAN HIGHBALL
3 oz. Tullamore Dew
2 tsp. Pineapple Juice
1 tsp. Lemon Juice
Club Soda
Combine the whiskey with the juices; add ice and fill with soda. Stir gently.

HOT IRISH
1 1/4 oz. Tullamore Dew
1-2 tsp. Sugar
1 slice Fresh Lemon
4 Cloves
pinch Cinnamon or Cinnamon Stick
3-4 oz. Boiling Water
Stud lemon slice with cloves. Put lemon slice, sugar and cinnamon into stemmed glass. Add boiling water and Irish Whiskey. Stir and serve.

HOT IRISH AND PORT
1 1/2 oz. Bushmills Irish Whiskey
2 oz. Port
2 oz. Water
Pour into saucepan. Heat to boiling point but do not boil. Pour into mug. Add cinnamon stick and orange slice.

HOT MIST
2 parts Irish Mist
1 part Boiling Water
Garnish with slice of lemon and cloves. Serve in a goblet glass.

HOT TODDY
1 1/4 oz. Jameson Premium Imported Whiskey
1/2 slice Fresh Lemon
4 Cloves
2 tsp. Brown Sugar
pinch Cinnamon
Boiling Water
Stud lemon slice with cloves. Put lemon, sugar and cinnamon into warm cup or glass. Add boiling water and Jameson Premium Imported Whiskey. Stir well and serve.

ICY BRENDAN'S
3 oz. Saint Brendan's Superior Irish Cream
2 scoops Vanilla Ice cream
Blend until frothy.

INNISFREE FIZZ
2 oz. Irish Whiskey
1 oz. Lemon Juice
1 oz. Curacao
1/2 oz. Sugar Syrup or to taste
Club Soda
Mix all ingredients except club soda with cracked ice in a shaker or blender. Strain into a chilled wine goblet and fill with club soda.

INSPIRATION
1/4 Cork Dry Gin
1/4 Dry Vermouth
1/4 Calvados
1/4 Grand Marnier
Mix. Add a cherry.

INTERNATIONAL COFFEE

1/2 oz. Devonshire
1/2 oz. Chambord
Hot Coffee
Serve in a mug.

INTERNATIONAL CREAM

1/2 shot Carolans Irish Cream
1/2 shot Coffee-flavored Liqueur (Kahlua)
splash Grand Marnier
2 scoops Vanilla Ice Cream
splash Milk
Blend.

IRISH ANGEL

3/4 oz. Jameson Irish Whiskey
1/4 oz. Light Creme de Cacao
1/4 oz. White Creme de Menthe
1 1/2 oz. Heavy Cream
Shake well with crushed ice. Strain into chilled
cocktail glass or serve on the rocks.

IRISH APPLE

2 parts Carolans Irish Cream
1 part Laird's Apple Jack
Stir well on the rocks.

IRISH CANADIAN

1/2 oz. Irish Mist
1 1/2 oz. Canadian Whiskey
In a mixing glass half-filled with ice cubes combine both of the ingredients. Stir well. Strain into a cocktail glass.

IRISH CANDY

3 oz. Baileys Original Irish Cream
1 1/4 oz. Chocolate Raspberry Liqueur
1 oz. White Creme de Cacao
Build over ice. Stir and serve.

IRISH CELEBRATION

1 1/4 oz. Bushmills
1/4 oz. Green Creme de Menthe
splash Champagne
Shake ingredients with ice and strain into a large wine glass; top with champagne.

IRISH CHARLIE

1/2 shot Carolans Irish Cream
1/2 shot White Creme de Menthe
Shake with ice. Serve in a shot glass.

IRISH COLA

1 shot Baileys Irish Cream
Fill with Cola; garnish with cherry. Serve in rocks/old-fashioned glass.

IRISH COLLINS

Fill goblet with ice
juice of a small lemon
one spoon of powdered sugar
one jigger of Irish Whiskey.
Strain into large thin glass and fill with one bottle
of soda. Stir with spoon.

IRISH COOLER

1 1/4 oz. Tullamore Dew
6 oz. Club Soda
Pour whiskey into a highball glass over ice cubes.
Top with soda and stir. Garnish with a lemon peel
spiral.

IRISH COW

1 1/2 oz. Tullamore Dew
8 oz. Hot Milk
1 tsp. Sugar
Pour the milk into a glass; add the sugar and
whiskey. Stir well.

IRISH COWBOY

1 part Baileys Original Irish Cream
1 part Bourbon
Shake or stir on the rocks.

IRISH CREAM STINGER

3 parts Carolans Irish Cream
1 part White Creme de Menthe
Stir well on the rocks.

IRISH CRESTA

1 oz. Tullamore Dew
2 tsp. Irish Mist
2 tsp. Orange Juice
1 Egg White
Combine with ice; shake well. Strain and add ice.

IRISH DELIGHT

1 1/2 oz. Bushmills Irish Whiskey
3/4 oz. Cream
In a rocks glass with ice. Stir.

IRISH DOWN UNDER

1 part Baileys Original Irish Cream
1 part Stubbs Australian Rum
Shake with ice and serve.

IRISH DREAM

1/2 oz. Carolans Irish Cream
1/2 oz. Hazelnut Liqueur
1/2 oz. Dark Creme de Cacao
1 scoop Vanilla Ice Cream
Combine ingredients in a blender with ice. Blend
thoroughly. Pour into a collins or parfait glass.
Serve with a straw.

IRISH EYES

1 oz. Kilbeggan Irish Whiskey
1/4 oz. Green Creme de Menthe
2 oz. Heavy Cream
Shake well with crushed ice. Strain into chilled
cocktail glass. Garnish with maraschino cherry.

IRISH EYES #2

1 1/2 oz. Saint Brendan's Superior Irish Cream
1 1/2 oz. Cream
splash Cola
splash Soda Water
Serve long and tall over ice.

IRISH FIX #1

2 oz. Jameson Irish Whiskey
2 tsp. Irish Mist
2 tsp. Lemon Juice
1 tsp. Sugar
Dissolve the sugar with a few drops of hot water in a
glass. Add whiskey and lemon juice; fill with
crushed ice and stir well. Add slices of orange and
lemon and float the Irish Mist on top.

IRISH FIX #2

2 oz. Tullamore Dew
1/2 oz. Irish Mist
1 oz. Pineapple Juice
1/2 oz. Lemon Juice
1/2 tsp. Sugar Syrup
Fill mixing glass with ice.
Add Irish Whiskey, Irish Mist,pineapple juice,
lemon juice and sugar syrup. Shake. Strain into a
rocks glass filled with ice. Garnish with lemon slice.

IRISH FIZZ

2 1/2 oz. Tullamore Dew
1 1/2 tsp. Lemon Juice
1 tsp. Triple Sec
1/2 tsp. Sugar
Club Soda
Combine (except the soda) with ice; shake. Strain; add ice and club soda.

IRISH FLAG SHOOTER

1 oz. Green Creme de Menthe
1 oz. Carolans Irish Cream
1 oz. Grand Marnier
Pour ingredients in order given into a pousse-cafe or cordial glass so that they form separate layers.

IRISH FROG

3/4 oz. Midori
3/4 oz. Baileys Irish Cream (chilled)
1 1/2 oz. Cordial glass.
Layer in above order.

IRISH FROST SHOOTER

1 shot Baileys Irish Cream
1 splash Coco Lopez Cream of Coconut
1 splash Half & Half
Shake and strain. Garnish with cinnamon. Serve in pony/cordial glass.

IRISH HEADLOCK

1/4 oz. Carolans Irish Cream
1/4 oz. Irish Whiskey
1/4 oz. Amaretto
1/4 oz. Brandy
Layer in above order.

IRISH HORSEMAN

3/4 oz. Jameson Irish Whiskey
1/4 oz. Triple Sec
3 oz. Sweet & Sour Mix
8 oz. Crushed Ice
1/4 oz. Chambord
Combine whiskey, triple sec and sweet & sour mix
with crushed ice. Shake well. Pour into highball
glass. Top with raspberry liqueur.

IRISH KILT

1 oz. Kilbeggan Irish Whiskey
1 oz. Scotch
1 oz. Lemon Juice
1 1/2 oz. Sugar Syrup or to taste
Several dashes Orange Bitters
Mix all ingredients with cracked ice in a shaker or
blender and strain into a chilled cocktail glass.

IRISH KISS

3/4 oz. Tullamore Dew
1/2 oz. Peach Schnapps
4 oz. Ginger Ale
2 oz. Orange Juice
Combine in an ice cube-filled Collins or specialty
glass. Garnish with lime wheel.

IRISH KNIGHT

2 oz. Bushmills Irish Whiskey
2 dashes Noilly Prat Dry Vermouth
2 dashes Benedictine
In an old-fashioned glass add twist of orange peel.

IRISH LACED

1 shot Irish Mist
2 splashes Coco Lopez Cream of Coconut
2 splashes Half & Half
3 splashes Pineapple Juice
2 scoops Ice
Blend. Garnish with orange flag. Serve in hurricane/poco glass.

IRISH MAGIC

1 oz. Jameson Irish Whiskey
1/4 oz. White Creme de Cacao
5 oz. Orange Juice
Pour all ingredients over ice in a glass. Stir.

IRISH MARTINI

1 oz. Bushmills
1 oz. Baileys
Shake with ice and strain into a martini glass
with dark chocolate shavings on top.

IRISH MIST ALEXANDER

1 oz. Irish Mist
1 oz. Light Cream
1 oz. Dark Creme de Cacao
Shake ingredients with cracked ice. Strain into
cocktail glass. Sprinkle with nutmeg.

IRISH MIST COFFEE

1 part Irish Mist
Coffee
Pour into a coffee glass. Stir. Top with whipped cream. No sugar needed.

IRISH MIST KISS

1 part Irish Mist
dash Hiram Walker Blue Curacao
splash Soda
Serve in a rocks glass with ice.

IRISH MIST SODA

1 part Irish Mist
3 parts Club Soda
Serve with ice and wedge of lime or lemon in a tall glass. Garnish with fruit.

IRISH MIST SOUR

2 parts Irish Mist
1 part Lemon Juice or Sour Mix
Shake well over ice. Serve in a tall glass. Garnish with fruit.

IRISH MIST STRAIGHT

or on the rocks
1 1/2 oz. Irish Mist
What could be better than the pure taste of either straight up or over ice? Say no more. Serve in a snifter or on the rocks.

IRISH NIGHT CAP

1 1/2 oz. Jameson Irish Whiskey
4 oz. Hot Milk
1 tsp. Sugar
Pour milk into glass add sugar and Bushmills; stir
well.

IRISH PENANCE

1 part Carolans Irish Cream
1 part Cointreau
Shake slowly and serve on the rocks.

IRISH POT OF GOLD

1 oz. Devonshire Irish Cream
1/2 oz. Goldschlager
Serve over ice.

IRISH PRINCE

1 1/4 oz. Jameson Irish Whiskey
3 oz. Tonic Water
In an old-fashioned glass add ice cubes and stir
gently. Drop in lemon peel.

IRISH QUAALUDE

1/2 oz. Baileys Irish Cream
1/2 oz. Absolut
1/2 oz. Frangelico
1/2 oz. White Creme de Cacao
Shaker can 1/2 ice. Put recipe into can. Shake
and strain.

IRISH RAINBOW

1 1/2 oz. Irish Whiskey
Several dashes Pernod
Several dashes Curacao
Several dashes Maraschino Liqueur
Several dashes Angostura Bitters
Orange Peel
Mix all ingredients except orange peel with cracked ice in a shaker or blender. Pour into a chilled old-fashioned glass. Twist orange peel over drink and drop in.

IRISH RASPBERRY

1 oz. Devonshire Irish Cream
1/2 oz. Chambord
Blend with 1 cup of ice.

IRISH RICKEY

1 1/2 oz. Tullamore Dew
1 cube Ice
Juice of 1/2 Lime
Fill 8 oz. highball glass with carbonated water and stir. Leave lime in glass.

IRISH ROSE

1 jigger Irish Whiskey
3-4 dashes Grenadine
1 lump Ice
Fill glass from soda siphon.

IRISH RUSSIAN

1 part Carolans Irish Cream
1 part Vodka
Stir well on the rocks.

IRISH SHILLELAH

1 1/2 oz. Jameson Irish Whiskey
Juice of 1/2 Lemon
1 tsp. Powdered Sugar
1/2 oz. Sloe Gin
1/2 oz. Rum
2 slices Peach
Shake well with cracked ice and strain into 5 oz.
punch glass. Decorate with fresh raspberries,
strawberries and a cherry.

IRISH SLING

In an old-fashioned glass mix:
1 jigger Tullamore Dew
1 jigger Gin
Crush one lump of sugar and two lumps of ice
and add to glass.

IRISH SOUR

1 1/2 oz. Jameson Irish Whiskey
Juice of 1/2 Lemon
1 tsp. Sugar
Shake vigorously with ice until frothy. Stir into
sour glass; add a maraschino cherry and
orange slice.

IRISH SPRING

1 oz. Jameson Irish Whiskey
1/2 oz. Peach Schnapps
1 oz. Orange Juice
1 oz. Sweet & Sour
In a collins glass with ice; stir well. Garnish with orange slice and cherry.

IRISH STING

1 1/2 oz. Bushmills Irish Whiskey
1/4 oz. White Creme de Menthe
Shake. Serve up or on the rocks.

IRISH SUMMER COFFEE

1 oz. Irish Whiskey
1/4 oz. Carolans Irish Cream
4 oz. Cold Coffee
Stir with cubed ice. Strain into wineglass or specialty coffee glass. Garnish with whipped cream if desired.

IRISH SURFER

1 1/4 oz. Irish Mist
3 oz. Orange Juice
Sugar
Club Soda
Shake Irish Mist, orange juice and sugar. Top with club soda.

IRISH WAKE-UP

3 oz. Irish Whiskey
1 tsp. Sugar
4 Whole Cloves
2 Tbsp. Heavy Cream
1 Teaspoon
1 cup Steaming Fresh Coffee
Grated Nutmeg

Fill tall, heatproof glass with coffee. Add Irish Whiskey, sugar, and cloves and place teaspoon in glass. When teaspoon has heated to same temperature as contents, hold it just under surface and slowly pour cream into teaspoon in glass (this should float the cream without mixing it). Sprinkle nutmeg on top.

IRISH WHISKEY COOLER

1 jigger Tullamore Dew
1 pint Club Soda
1 dash Angostura Bitters
1 Lemon Rind

Serve in tall glass.

IRISH WHISKEY FIZ

1 jigger Jameson Irish Whiskey
1 barspoon Sugar
Juice of Lemon

Shake, strain into fizz glass. Fill glass from soda siphon.

IRISH WHISKEY PUNCH

Juice of lime
One lump of ice
Add Irish Whiskey to taste. Fill glass with carbonated mineral water. Stir with spoon.

IRISH WHISKEY SOUR

1 jigger Tullamore Dew
Juice of lemon
1 barspoon Sugar
Shake. Strain into sour glass or serve on the rocks. Dress with fruit (orange slice and cherry).

IRISH-CANADIAN SANGAREE

2 tsp. Irish Mist
1 1/4 oz. Canadian Whiskey
1 tsp. Orange Juice
1 tsp. Lemon Juice
Combine and stir well. Add ice and dust with nutmeg.

J.J.'S SHAMROCK

1 oz. Irish Whiskey
1/2 oz. White Creme de Cacao
1/2 oz. Green Creme de Menthe
1 oz. Milk
Mix in a shaker or blender with cracked ice and serve in a chilled cocktail glass.

JAGER SHAKE

1/5 shot Irish Cream
1/5 shot Jagermeister
1/5 shot Root Beer Schnapps
1/5 shot Amaretto
1/5 shot Cola
Shake with ice. Serve as a shot.

JAMESON JEWEL

2 parts Jameson Premium Imported Whiskey
6 parts Pineapple Juice
4 parts Peach Schnapps
dash Blue Curacao
Shake with ice and serve over ice or straight up.

JAVA COW

1 part O'Mara's Irish Country Cream
1 part Copa de Oro Coffee Liqueur
1 part Burnett's Vodka
Shake together well; pour over ice.

JELLYFISH

1/4 shot Carolans Irish Cream
1/4 shot White Creme de Cacao
1/4 shot Amaretto
1/4 shot Grenadine
Pour first three ingredients directly into glass.
Pour grenadine in center of glass.

JOHN'S DELIGHT
6/10 Cork Dry Gin
2/10 Orange Juice
2/10 Cointreau
Egg White
Float Fresh Cream
Shake all except cream. Float cream.

KERRY COOLER
2 oz. Tullamore Dew
1 1/2 oz. Sherry
1 1/4 Tbsp. Creme de Almond
1 1/4 Tbsp. Lemon Juice
Club Soda
Combine (except the soda) with ice, shake well.
Strain, add ice and soda. Top with a lemon slice.

KINSALE COOLER
1 1/2 oz. Irish Whiskey
1 oz. Irish Mist
1 oz. Lemon Juice
Club Soda
Ginger Ale
Lemon Peel
Mix Irish Whiskey, Irish Mist, lemon juice with
cracked ice in a shaker or blender. Pour into a
chilled collins glass. Fill with equal parts of club
soda and ginger ale. Stir gently. Twist lemon peel
over drink and drop in.

KISS ME KATE

1 part Saint Brendan's Superior Irish Cream
1 part Creme de Cacao
1/2 part Raspberry Liqueur
Serve as a shooter or over ice.

KOALA HUG

1 1/4 oz. Jameson Irish Whiskey
2 oz. Lemon Juice
1 oz. Cointreau
dash Pernod
Shaken with ice. Method: tall glass, ice cubes,
slice of orange/lemon, straws.

KRAZY KANGAROO

1 1/4 oz. Jameson Irish Whiskey
dash Pernod
2 oz. Orange Juice
Pour into mixing glass. Method: ice, stir, decorate
with orange rind.

L'IL ORPHAN ANNIE

A 4-oz cocktail glass, chilled
1 1/2 oz. Irish Whiskey
1 oz. Baileys Irish Cream
2 Tbsp. Chocolate-flavored Ovaltine powder (or 1
Tbsp. chocolate syrup)
1 tsp. Shaved Chocolate
Combine all ingredients except shaved chocolate
in shaker and shake vigorously. Strain into glass.
Garnish with shaved chocolate.

LEPRECHAUN

2 oz. Tullamore Dew
3 oz. Tonic Water
3-4 Ice Cubes
Twist Lemon Peel
Put whiskey and tonic water in an old-fashioned glass, add ice cubes and stir gently. Drop in the lemon peel. Serves 1.

LEPRECHAUN'S CHOICE

1 1/4 oz. Baileys Original Irish Cream
3/4 oz. Smirnoff Vodka
Club Soda
Serve in tall glass. Top with club soda.

LEPRECHAUN'S LIBATION

2 1/2 oz. Old Bushmills Irish Whiskey
1 oz. Green Creme de Menthe
Fill blender with 3 1/2 oz. cracked ice. Add green Creme de Menthe and Old Bushmills Irish Whiskey. Blend. Pour into a goblet or large wine glass. (Courtesy of Beach Grill, Westminster, Colorado)

LIMP MOOSE

1/2 shot Carolans Irish Cream
1/2 shot Canadian Club
Chill.

MAIDEN'S PRAYER
3/8 Cork Dry Gin
3/8 Cointreau
1/8 Orange Juice
1/8 Lemon Juice
Shake with ice.

MALIBU SLIDE
Equal Parts:
Baileys Original Irish Cream
Kahlua
Malibu
Blend with ice.

MEADE SPRITZER
2 oz. Bunratty Meade
Club Soda
Ice
Lemon Slice
Serve in tall glass with ice.

MEXICAROLANS
1 part Carolans Irish Cream
1 part Tequila
Shake well with ice and serve on the rocks.

MILK & HONEY
Equal Parts:
Irish Mist
Carolans Irish Cream
Serve in a rocks glass.

MINGLING OF THE CLANS
1 1/4 oz. Bushmills Irish Whiskey
1/2 oz. Scotch
2 tsp. Lemon Juice
3 dashes Orange Bitters
In a mixing glass with ice. Strain into cocktail glass.

MIST OLD FASHIONED
1 1/4 oz. Irish Mist
Orange slice
cherry bitters
sugar
soda or water
Muddle orange, cherry, bitters and sugar. Add Irish Mist. Top with soda or water.

MISTER MURPHY
1 part Irish Mist
1 part White Rum
1 part Orange Juice
Serve in a rocks glass with a dash of Angostura Bitters.

MISTY MIST
1 1/4 oz. Irish Mist
Serve on shaved ice.

MISTY-EYED IRISHMAN

3/4 oz. Bushmills Irish Whiskey
1 oz. Peppermint Schnapps
1 pkg. Hot Chocolate Mix
Optional: Sprinkle with candy mint shavings
Fill with hot coffee, stir well. Top with whipped cream.

MONKEY SEE - MONKEY DO

1 part Baileys Original Irish Cream
1 part Rhum Barbancourt
1 part Banana Liqueur
1 part Orange Juice
Shake with ice and serve.

MS. TEA

1 1/4 oz. Irish Mist
3 oz. Iced Tea
Mix. Serve on the rocks.

MUDSLIDE

1 part each
Baileys Original Irish Cream
Kahlua
Vodka
Mix and pour. Also delicious blended with ice and served as a frozen beverage.

MURPHY'S DREAM
1 part Irish Mist
1 part Gin
1 part Lemon Juice
Sugar
Shake. Serve up or on the rocks.

NEGRONI
1/3 Cork Dry Gin
1/3 Sweet Vermouth
1/3 Campari
On the rocks. Garnish with 1/2 slice of orange,
soda if desired. Mix.

NELLIE JANE
1 1/4 oz. Irish Mist
1/4 oz. Hiram Walker Peach Schnapps
3 oz. Orange Juice
1 oz. Ginger Ale
Mix all but ginger ale. Float ginger ale.

NUT N' HOLLI
1/4 Irish Mist
1/4 Amaretto
1/4 Carolans Irish Cream
1/4 Frangelico
Shake. Serve straight up in a shot glass.

NUTTY IRISHMAN
1/2 shot Carolans Irish Cream
1/2 shot Hazelnut Liqueur (Frangelico)
Serve as a shot or on the rocks.

NUTTY PROFESSOR
1/3 shot Carolans Irish Cream
1/3 shot Hazelnut Liqueur (Frangelico)
1/3 shot Grand Marnier
Serve as a shot or on the rocks.

O'CASEY'S SCOTCH TERRIER
1 part Baileys Original Irish Cream
1 part J&B Scotch
Stir well on the rocks.

O.J. MIST
1 part Irish Mist
3 parts Orange Juice
Serve in a tall glass.

OATMEAL COOKIE
Equal parts:
Baileys Original Irish Cream
Goldschlager
Butterscotch Schnapps
Serve as a shot.

OLD ETONIAN
1/2 Cork Dry Gin
1/2 Lillet
2 dashes Orange Bitters
2 dashes Creme de Noyeaux
Mix with ice. Serve with orange peel.

ORGASM

1/3 shot Irish Cream
1/3 shot Amaretto
1/3 shot Kahlua
Serve as a shot.

ORIENTAL RUG

1/4 shot Carolans Irish Cream
1/4 shot Hazelnut Liqueur (Frangelico)
1/4 shot Jagermeister
1/4 shot Coffee-flavored Liqueur (Kahlua)
dash Cola
Serve as a shot.

PADDY COCKTAIL

1 1/2 oz. Tullamore Dew
3/4 oz. Sweet Vermouth
Several dashes Angostura Bitters
Mix all ingredients with cracked ice in a shaker or
blender. Serve in a chilled cocktail glass.

PADDY COCKTAIL/IRISH MANHATTAN

1 1/4 oz. Paddy Irish Whiskey
1 1/4 oz. Dry Vermouth
1 dash Angostura Bitters
Stir well with cracked ice and strain into 3 oz.
cocktail glass.

PADDY O'ROCCO
1 1/2 oz. Irish Mist
3 oz. Orange Juice
splash Amaretto
Mix Irish Mist and orange juice. Top with splash of Amaretto.

PADDY'S WAGON
An old-fashioned glass
chilled
1 1/2 oz. Irish Whiskey
1 1/2 oz. Sweet Vermouth
1-2 dashes Angostura Bitters
1-2 dashes Southern Comfort
5-7 Ice Cubes
Combine all ingredients except 2 to 3 ice cubes in shaker and shake vigorously. Place remaining ice in glass and strain drink into glass.

PARKNASILLA PEG LEG
1 1/2 oz. Irish Whiskey
1 oz. Coconut Syrup
3 oz. Pineapple Juice
1 tsp. Lemon Juice
Club Soda
Mix whiskey, coconut syrup, and fruit juices in a shaker or blender with cracked ice and pour into a chilled highball glass along with several ice cubes. Fill with club soda. Stir gently.

PATTY'S PRIDE

1 oz. Irish Whiskey
1/4 oz. Peppermint Schnapps
1 oz. Club Soda
Combine in an ice cube filled old-fashioned glass.

PATTY'S PRIDE

1 1/4 oz. Bushmills Irish Whiskey
1/4 oz. Peppermint Schnapps
Serve on the rocks.

PAUL HEFFERNAN'S COCKTAIL
JAMESON'S JEWEL

Ireland's entry to the International Cocktail
Competition
Tokyo: October 9-13, 1996
2 cl Jameson Irish Whiskey
6 cl Pineapple Juice Britvic
4 cl Peach Schnapps
Top with 10 cl Bitter Lemon and dash (1 cl) Bols
Blue Curacao.
Note: cl = oz.

PEACH IRISH

1 1/2 oz. Irish Whiskey
1 Completely Ripe Peach, peeled, pitted and sliced
1/2 cup Fresh Lime Juice
1 oz. Apricot Brandy
1 Tbsp. Sugar, granulated, superfine (or to taste)
dash Vanilla
Mix peach, lime juice, Irish Whiskey, apricot
Brandy, sugar and vanilla for 10 seconds in
blender. Add 1 cup cracked ice and blend for
additional 15 seconds. Pour into chilled 12-oz.
glass, garnish with a twist and a slice of lime.
Makes 1 drink.

PICADILLY

2/3 Cork Dry Gin
1/3 Dry Vermouth
Dash Pernod
Dash Grenadine
Mix with ice and serve.

POET'S PUNCH

1 oz. Irish Mist
1 cup Milk
1 stick Cinnamon
twist Lemon
twist Orange
1/2 tsp. Vanilla
Heat milk, cinnamon stick, lemon and orange
twists to boiling point. Stir into remaining milk.
Add vanilla and Irish Mist. Strain. Sprinkle with
nutmeg.

PRINCESS MARY

1/3 Cork Dry Gin
1/3 Creme de Cacao
1/3 Fresh Cream
Shake with ice and serve.

R.A.C.

1/2 Cork Dry Gin
1/4 Dry Vermouth
1 Cherry and twist of Orange
Dash Orange bitters
Dash Grenadine
Mix with ice and serve.

RED DEVIL
2 oz. Tullamore Dew
1 1/2 oz. Clam Juice
1 1/2 oz. Tomato Juice
1 tsp. Lime Juice
Few drops Worchestershire Sauce
Pinch Pepper
Combine with ice; shake gently. Strain straight up.

RING OF KERRY
1 1/2 oz. Tullamore Dew
1 oz. Baileys Original Irish Cream
1/2 oz. Kahlua or Creme de Cacao
1 tsp. Shaved Chocolate
Mix all ingredients, except shaved chocolate, with cracked ice in a shaker or blender. Strain into a chilled cocktail glass. Sprinkle with shaved chocolate.

ROAD KILL
1/3 shot Jameson Irish Whiskey
1/3 shot Wild Turkey Whiskey
1/3 shot 151-proof Rum
Serve as a shot.

ROYAL ROMANCE
1/2 Cork Dry Gin
1/4 Grand Marnier
1/4 Dry Passion Fruit Juice
1 dash Sugar Syrup
Shake with ice and serve.

ROYAL SMILE
2/3 Cork Dry Gin
1/3 Calvados
3 dashes Sugar Syrup
3 dashes Lemon Juice
Shake with ice and serve.

RUDDY McDOWELL
An old-fashioned glass, chilled
1 1/2 oz. Irish Whiskey
2 oz. Tomato Juice
1 dash Tabasco Sauce
Freshly Ground Pepper, to taste
6-8 Ice Cubes
Combine all ingredients except 3 to 4 ice cubes in shaker and shake vigorously. Place remaining ice in glass and strain drink into glass.

SAN FRANCISCO
1/3 Cork Dry Gin
1/3 Dry Vermouth
1/3 Sweet Vermouth
Dash Orange Bitters
Dash Angostura
Mix with ice. Add a cherry.

SAN JUAN IRISHMAN
1 part Baileys Original Irish Cream
1 part Puerto Rican Rum
Shake with ice and serve on the rocks.

SCHNAPPY SHILLELAGH

2 parts Carolans Irish Cream
1 part Peppermint Schnapps
Stir well on the rocks.

SCOTCH IRISH

1 part Baileys Original Irish Cream
1 part J&B Scotch
Shake or stir on the rocks.

SCREAMING ORGASM

1/4 shot Irish Cream
1/4 shot Coffee-flavored Liqueur (Kahlua)
1/4 shot Vodka
1/4 shot Amaretto
Serve as a shot.

SEMINOLE

3/10 Cork Dry Gin
2/10 Bols Creme de Bananes
2/10 Midori Melon Liqueur
2/10 Pineapple Juice
1/10 Fresh Cream
Orange, Cherry Garnish
Shake.

SERPENT'S SMILE

An old-fashioned glass chilled
3/4 oz. Jameson Irish Whiskey
1 1/2 oz. Sweet Vermouth
3/4 oz. Lemon Juice
1 Tbsp. Kummel
2 dashes Angostura Bitters
5-7 Ice Cubes
1 strip Lemon Peel
Combine all ingredients except 2 to 3 ice cubes and lemon peel in shaker and shake vigorously. Place remaining ice in glass and strain drink into glass. Twist lemon peel over drink to release oil and drop it in.

SERPENT'S TOOTH

1 oz. Tullamore Dew
2 oz. Sweet Vermouth
1/2 oz. Kummel
1 oz. Lemon Juice
Dash Angostura Bitters
Stir well, strain into small wine glass.

SHAMROCK COCKTAIL

1 1/2 oz. Bushmills Irish Whiskey
1/2 oz. French Vermouth
1 tsp. Green Creme de Menthe
Stir well with cracked ice and strain into 3 oz. cocktail glass. Serve with an olive.

SHAMROCK No. 1

1 1/2 oz. Jameson Irish Whiskey
3/4 oz. Dry Vermouth
1 tsp. Green Chartreuse
1 tsp. Green Creme de Menthe
Stir all ingredients with plenty of ice in a pitcher
and strain into a chilled cocktail glass.

SHAMROCK No. 2

1 1/2 oz. Bushmills Irish Whiskey
1 1/2 oz. Green Creme de Menthe
2 oz. Heavy Cream
Maraschino Cherry
Mix all ingredients except cherry with cracked ice
in a shaker or blender. Pour into a chilled old-
fashioned glass. Garnish with maraschino cherry.

SHAMROCK No. 3

1 1/2 oz. Busmills Irish Whiskey
3/4 oz. Green Creme de Menthe
4 oz. Vanilla Ice Cream
Mix all ingredients in a blender at high speed until
smooth. Pour into a chilled wine goblet.

SHETLAND PONY

1 1/2 oz. Scotch
3/4 oz. Irish Mist
dash Orange Bitters (optional)
Mix all ingredients with cracked ice in a mixing
glass and strain into a chilled cocktail glass.

SIFI FLIP

1/2 Cork Dry Gin
1/4 Cointreau
1/4 Grenadine
Juice of 1/2 Lemon
Yolk of Egg
Shake with ice and strain.

SILVER SHAMROCK

2 parts Bunratty Meade
1 part Vodka
Stir with ice.

SIXTY-NINTH (69TH) REGIMENT PUNCH

(Use a hot whiskey glass)
1/2 wine glass Irish Whiskey
1/2 wine glass Scotch Whisky
1 tsp. Sugar
2-3 dashes Lemon Juice
2 wine glasses Hot water
Imbibing the above adds greatly to one's comfort
on a cold night.

SKIBBEREEN TONIC

2 oz. Irish Whiskey
Tonic Water
Lemon Peel
Pour Irish Whiskey into a chilled old-fashioned
glass with several ice cubes. Fill with tonic water.
Twist lemon peel over drink and drop in.

SLIPPERY NUT

1 1/2 oz. Saint Brendan's Superior Irish Cream
2 oz. Roncoco Rum Liqueur
Serve over ice.

SOUTH WIND

3/10 Cork Dry Gin
3/10 Peach Schnapps
3/10 Orange Juice
1/10 Cream
Shake with ice and serve. Garnish with orange
slice and cherry.

SOUTHERN DELIGHT

1/4 Cork Dry Gin
1/4 Southern Comfort
1/4 Baileys Irish Cream
1/4 Pure Orange Juice
Mint leaves, cherries, lemon.
Shake with ice. Garnish with mint leaves, cherry
and lemon.

SPEARAMISTY

1 oz. Irish Mist
1/4 oz. Spearmint Schnapps
Mix. Serve up or on the rocks.

ST. PATRICK'S DAY COCKTAIL

3/4 oz. Bushmills Irish Whiskey
3/4 oz. Green Creme de Menthe
3/4 oz. Green Chartreuse
1 dash Angostura Bitters
Stir well with cracked ice and strain into 3 oz.
cocktail glass.

SUNSET DREAM

1 1/2 oz. Cork Dry Gin
1/2 oz. Creme de Cacao
dash Grenadine
Pouring Cream
Shake with ice. Top with whipped cream and
strawberry.

SWEET IRISH STORM

1 1/2 oz. Bushmills Irish Whiskey
3/4 oz. Noilly Prat Sweet French Vermouth
Several dashes Angostura Bitters
Several dashes Southern Comfort
Mix ingredients with cracked ice in shaker or
blender. Pour into chilled old-fashioned glass.

TANGO

1/2 Cork Dry Gin
1/4 Sweet Vermouth
1/4 Dry Vermouth
2 dashes Orange Curacao
Dash Orange Juice
Shake with ice.

TARZAN O'REILLY

1 oz. Baileys Original Irish Cream
1/2 oz. Smirnoff Vodka
1/2 oz. Creme de Banana
Build in shot glass over ice. Stir.

TERMINATOR

1/5 shot Irish Cream
1/5 shot Coffee-flavored liqueur (Kahlua)
1/5 shot Sambuca
1/5 shot Grand Marnier
1/5 shot Vodka
Layer.

THE BRANDYWINE

2 parts Bunratty Meade
1 part Brandy
Stir with ice.

THE GREAT WHITE

1 1/4 oz. Jameson Irish Whiskey
2 oz. Apple Juice
1 oz. White Curacao
Pour into glass. Method: Ice in tall glass, decorate
with slice of apple/orange, sprig of mint and
straw.

THE HONEYMOONER

2 parts Bunratty Meade
1 part Amaretto
1 part Cream
Shake and pour over ice. Garnish with cinnamon.

THE ULTIMATE IRISH COFFEE

1 1/2 oz. Irish Mist
Hot Coffee
The superior taste of Irish Mist is combined with coffee and topped with whipped cream to make the ultimate Irish Coffee. Serve in a warm mug. No sugar needed.

THE ULTIMATE TEA

1 1/2 oz. Irish Mist
Hot Tea
A bit of lemon
Indulge yourself with this hot new taste. The ULTIMATE IRISH TEA made exclusively with IRISH MIST. Serve in a warm mug. No sugar needed.

THREE-LEAF SHAMROCK SHAKER

1 oz. Bushmills Irish Whiskey
1 oz. Light Rum
1 oz. Brandy
1 tsp. Lemon Juice
Sugar Syrup to taste
Shake ingredients with cracked ice. Strain into chilled glass.

TINKER'S TEA

1 1/2 oz. Baileys Original Irish Cream
Hot Tea
Pour Baileys in mug or cup. Fill with hot tea.

TIPPERARY

1 oz. Jameson Irish Whiskey
1/2 oz. Noilly Prat Sweet Vermouth
1/4 oz. Green Chartreuse
Combine with 4 to 5 ice cubes in mixing glass and
stir well. Strain into glass.

TO THE MOON

1/4 shot Irish Cream
1/4 shot Amaretto
1/4 shot Coffee-flavored liqueur (Kahlua)
1/4 shot 151-proof Rum
Serve as a shot.

TOASTED BRENDAN'S

1/2 oz. Saint Brendan's Superior Irish Cream
1/2 oz. Coffee Liqueur
1/2 oz. Amaretto
Fill with Coffee. Top with whipped cream.

TOASTED IRISHMAN

1 part Irish Mist
1 part Kahlua
1 part Di Saronno Amaretto
Shake with ice and serve on the rocks.

TOOTSIE ROLL

1/2 oz. Baileys Original Irish Cream
1 oz. Root Beer Schnapps
Topped with dash of Baileys Irish Cream.

U-Z

3/4 oz. Irish Mist
3/4 oz. Baileys Irish Cream
3/4 oz. Kahlua
Shaker can 1/2 ice. Put recipe into can. Shake and strain.

VULCAN MIND PROBE

1/3 shot Carolans Irish Cream
1/3 shot Peppermint Schnapps
1/3 shot 151-proof Rum
Large Drinking Straw
Layer. Suck drink down through straw in one gulp.

WHITE LADY

1/2 Cork Dry Gin
1/4 Lemon Juice
1/4 Cointreau
Dash Egg White
Shake with ice. Serve on the rocks.

WICKLOW COOLER

1 1/2 oz. Jameson Irish Whiskey
1 oz. Jamaican Dark Rum
1/2 oz. Lime Juice
1 oz. Orange Juice
1 tsp. Falernum or Orgeat Syrup
Ginger Ale
Mix all ingredients except ginger ale with cracked ice in a shaker or blender. Pour into a chilled collins glass. Fill with ginger ale.

WILD IRISH ROSE
1 1/2 oz. Tullamore Dew
1 1/2 tsp. Grenadine
1/2 oz. Lime Juice
Club Soda
Fill a highball glass with ice. Add Irish Whiskey, grenadine and lime juice. Stir well. Fill with club soda.

WOLFHOUND
1 oz. Bushmills
3/4 oz. Dark Creme de Cacao
1/2 oz. Half & Half
splash Club Soda
Shake with ice, top with club soda.

XIANTHA
1/3 Cork Dry Gin
1/3 Yellow Chartreuse
1/3 Cherry Brandy
Mix with ice.

YELLOW DAISY
2/5 Cork Dry Gin
2/5 Dry Vermouth
1/5 Grand Marnier
Mix with ice.

The Story of Irish Coffee

Irish Coffee, Ireland's gift to the list of great drinks of the world, is in fact a remarkably recent discovery.

Irish Whiskey has been Ireland's national spirit drink for more than 1,000 years, and the habit of putting whiskey into tea has been common ever since tea drinking became established in Ireland in the 16th century.

When transatlantic flying began again after the end of the Second World War, the aircraft of the time - flying boats and the earlier Super Constellations - could not make the entire Atlantic crossing without having to make refueling stops. The most important of these refueling stops was at Shannon Airport, on the western fringe of Ireland and Europe, the last westbound stop before Gander in Newfoundland.

When these aircraft landed in Shannon Airport, the passengers had to disembark during the refueling and were often in need of a bit of refueling themselves. Joe Sheridan was the Chief Barman at that time in Shannon Airport. He took the traditional old Irish drink - whiskey in tea - and dressed it up into a new and more glamorous form to be attractive to the Americans, who represented the majority of the travelers at that time. He substituted coffee for tea, since coffee was more to the American taste, added sugar, stirred well to dissolve the sugar, and then topped it off with a layer of fresh, lightly whipped Irish cream. Finally came his magic touch of serving the drink in a stemmed glass rather than in a cup, since the visual appeal of the contrast between the black coffee and the white cream was instantly attractive to the guests. He never served it with a spoon or a straw but encouraged the drinker to drink the hot coffee/whiskey through the cool cream. Joe Sheridan found that he had only to serve three or four Irish Coffees to the first few passengers to arrive in the Airport Bar, whereupon he would be immediately deluged with orders from the rest of them!

Because Shannon was truly a "gateway" between East and West, the fame of Irish Coffee spread very quickly. In America it soon became a favorite drink, and one restaurant in San Francisco - the Buena Vista on Fisherman's Wharf - claims to have been the first to popularize Irish Coffee in America: Stanton Delaplaine, a columnist for the San Francisco Chronicle brought the recipe for Irish Coffee to his favorite watering hole and publicized Irish Coffee unceasingly thereafter in his column. There is a bronze plaque fixed to the wall outside the Buena Vista's front door that records the fact that Irish Coffee was first served there. To this day it is a sight to see the staff of the Buena Vista preparing more than 2000 Irish Coffees every day! They are open 363 days of the year, closed only on Thanksgiving and Christmas Day.

The recipe also spread to Europe almost as quickly. Within a very short time Irish Coffee was being offered in all of Europe's top restaurants and bars, and it was established as a permanent favorite.

Today Irish Coffee is as popular as ever. Many consumers have their first ever taste of Irish Whiskey in this way. They move on later to enjoy the unique flavor of Irish Whiskey in its own right - with ice, with water or with soda - the world's original and the world's greatest whiskey.

There is a bronze plaque also in Shannon Airport, erected by the grateful whiskey distillers of Ireland, to record the fact that Irish Coffee was invented there by Joe Sheridan.

The recipe for Irish Coffee hasn't changed since Joe Sheridan's day, the original is still the best:

Into a stemmed glass, put two teaspoonfuls of sugar, preferably brown; add one-third Irish Whiskey and two-thirds really hot really strong black coffee, preferably freshly brewed, not instant. The glass should be filled with this mixture to within half an inch (1 cm) of the brim. Stir well at this point to ensure all of the sugar is dissolved, and then carefully float over the back of a spoon a collar of lightly-whipped cream, so that the cream floats on the top of the coffee and whiskey. Do not stir any more. Serve the drink without a spoon or a straw, as part of the pleasure comes from sipping the hot coffee and whiskey through the cool cream.

Slainte, agus saol agat! Health and long life to you!

Toasts & Wisdoms

"Health and long life to you,
Land without rent to you,
A child every year to you,
And may you die in Ireland."
Old Irish toast

To remember those who left
Irish shores never again to see
their homeland and to celebrate the
heritage and achievements of Irish
people around the world.
Slainte

Here's to health, peace, and prosperity;
May the flower of love never be
nipped by the frost of disappointment,
nor shadow of grief fall among a member
of this circle.
Here's to your health;
May God bring you luck
And may your journey be smooth and happy.
May you look back on the past with as much
pleasure as you look forward to the future.

May the road rise to meet you,
May the wind be always at your back,
The sun shine warm upon your face,
The rain fall soft upon your fields,
And until we meet again
May God hold you in the hollow of His hand.
Traditional Irish Toast

Mother's Day
to a wonderful mother who always has
...a smile for our joys
...a tear for our sorrows
...a comfort for our failings
...a prayer for our problems.
Here's to Mother—on her day!

Father's Day
To Dad—
from his children who acknowledge
their good fortune in being blessed
with a loving and dedicated father.

To our host, an excellent man;
For is not a man properly judged
by the company he keeps?

To the bride and groom—
May they have a lifetime of love
and an eternity of happiness.

To you on your anniversary:
May every new day bring more
happiness than yesterday.

Do not let your heart grow old
Though birthdays come and go;
To the youthful thoughts keep hold
Then, happiness you will know.
Happy Birthday.

May you live to be a hundred years
With one extra year to repent
Traditional Irish Toast

Let your boat of life be light
Packed with only what you need —
A homely home and simple pleasures,
One or two friends, worth the name,
Someone to love and someone to love you,
A cat, a dog, and a pipe or two,
Enough to eat and enough to wear,
And a little more than enough to drink...
For thirst is a dangerous thing.
Jerome K. Jerome, *Three Men in a Boat*

May good luck
be always your friend
Through life in all that you do
And may trouble be always
a stranger to you

Bless your little
Irish heart
and every other Irish part.

Here's to the health
of your enemies' enemies!

May the dust of your
carriage wheels
Blind the eyes of your foes.

May the roof above
you never fall in,
And your friends gathered below
never fall out.

The Irish Toast
"Slainte" (slauntca) - Cheers (health)

A Toast for an Irish Bachelor
May you have nicer legs
than yours under the table
before the new spuds are up.

We drink to your coffin,
May it be built
from the wood
Of a hundred year old
oak tree,
That I shall plant tomorrow.

Here's to health, peace,
and prosperity;
May the flower of Love never be
Nipped by the frost
of disappointment,
Nor shadow of grief
fall among
Your family or friends.

I drink to myself
and one other
And may that one other
be he
Who drinks to himself and one other
and may that one other be me!

May you _live_ all the
Days of your life.

Wishing you always:
Walls for the wind
And a roof for the rain
And tea beside the fire.
Laughter to cheer you.
And those you Love near you,
And all that your heart might desire.

May the light of heaven shine
On your grace.

"Slainthe Is Saul Agat" (slawne-cheh-iss sole-agat) —
Health and life to you!!

May you die in bed aged 100 years
Shot by a jealous husband.

May you live as long as you want
And never want as long as you live.

Here's to health to thine and thee
Not forgetting mine and me
When thine and thee next meet mine and me
May mine and me have as much welcome for thine and thee
As thine and thee have had for mine and me tonight.

May your doctor never earn a penny out of you
May your heart never give out
May the ten toes of your feet steer you clear of all misfortune
And before you're much older
May you hear much better toasts than this.

May the frost never afflict your spuds
May the outside leaves of your cabbage always
be free from worm
May the crows never pick at your haystack
And may your ass always be in foal.

May you be poor in misfortune
Rich in blessings
Slow to make enemies
Quick to make friends
But rich or poor
Quick or slow
May you know nothing but happiness
From this day forth.

May the wind be always at your back,
especially coming home on Saturday night.

May St. Peter never ask you to light a fire on a lake or advise
a headstrong woman.

May you always keep out from the priests;
that way you will keep in with them.

May you never stay seeing the bees
without spotting the honey.

May you dance with all the saints in
heaven bar St. Vitus.

May you be as well as you can bear to be.

May the hand that offer trouble be as idle
as the left hand of a bodhran.

May the lips that speak ill of you never say
thanks to St. Peter.

May your horse always stand in the middle of the fair.

Let your enemies hear the bees but
may you get the honey.

May you get what you're after with the help of God
and two policeman.

Hold your hour and have another!

Wet your whistle well and may we never
die of the drought!

Here's your health for consideration!

Drink up! It's always the next one that sickens you.

Good luck whatever!

Good health without a cold in your pipes!

Here's one for the road and
may you know every turning!

Here's mud in one eye and a glint in the other!

May the next drop make the grass grow long
on the road to hell for you!

Here's to the same again or something similar!

Good luck to you and bad shoes to your advisers.
(Said to a drinking companion who complains about drink
being bad for a man.)

Health! May your well never run dry!

Peace on your hand!

May God never knock you down
as long as you keep putting them up!

I'll give you your health and
may your enemies be beggars!

The face of the sad story be turned away from us!

Your life and your health to you!

Health to the man who buys his round
To heaven's alehouses be he bound.

Drink as if it was your last one but
may the last one not come till morning.

May God hold you in the hollow of His hand and
have a drink in the other for you.

May we keep a little of the fuel of youth to warm
our body in old age.

May you live to be a hundred—and
decide the rest for yourself.

You're not as young as you used to be
But you're not as old as you're going to be
So Watch it!

Here is to loving, to romance, to us.
May we travel together through time.
We alone count as none, but together we're one,
For our partnership puts love to rhyme.

A generation of children on the children of your children.

May he/she grow twice as tall as yourself and
half as wise.

May poverty always be a day's march behind us.

May the sunshine of comfort dispel the
clouds of despair.

Here's to you! No matter how old you are,
you don't look it!

Many happy returns of the day of your birth;
Many blessings to brighten your pathway on earth;
Many friendships to cheer and provoke you to mirth;
Many feastings and frolics to add to your girth.

Robert H. Lord

A Christmas wish—
May you never forget
what is worth remembering
or remember
what is best forgotten.

Holly and ivy hanging up
And something wet in every cup.

May you be as contented as Christmas finds you
all the year round.

May you be poor in misfortune this Christmas
and rich in blessings
slow to make enemies
quick to make friends
and rich or poor, slow or quick,
as happy as the New Year is long.

May you be the first house in the parish to
welcome St. Nicholas.

May your corn stand high as yourself, your fields
grow bigger with rain, and the mare know
its own way home on Christmas night.

May your sheep all have lambs
but not on Christmas night.

Peace and plenty for many a Christmas to come.

Friendship's the wine of life.
Let's drink of it and to it.

Here's all that's fine to you!
Books and old wine to you!
Girls be divine to you!
                    Richard Hovey

Here's to a friend. He knows you well and
likes you just the same.

To our best friends, who know the worst about us
but refuse to believe it.

May the clouds in your life form only a background
for a lovely sunset.

May we be happy and our enemies know it.

May we never feel want, nor ever want feeling.

May you always distinguish between the weeds and
the flowers.
May you be merry and lack nothing.
                                        Shakespeare

May the good Lord take a liking to you—but
not too soon.

May the holy Saints be about your bed, and about your
board, from this time to the latter end—God help us all!

The health of the salmon to you:
a long life,
a full heart
and a wet mouth!

May the path to hell grow green
for lack of travelers.

May the rocks in your field turn to gold.

May time never turn your head gray.

May you be seven times better off a year from now.

May your fire never go out.

May your well never run dry.

To a full moon on a dark night
And the road downhill all the way to your door.

To a warm bed, a dry stool, and glass in your window.

To the thirst that is yet to come.

Here's to love and unity,
Dark corners and opportunity.

Here's to Love, that begins with a fever and
ends with a yawn.

Here's to you who halves my sorrows and
doubles my joys.

Let's drink to love,
Which is nothing—
Unless it's divided by two.

May love draw the curtain and friendship the cork.

May we kiss those we please
And please those we kiss.

May we love as long as we live, and
live as long as we love.

As we start the New Year,
Let's get down on our knees
to thank God we're on our feet.

In the New Year,
may your right hand always be stretched out in friendship,
but never in want.

May the New Year bring summer in its wake.

Fat cattle, green fields, and
many a bushel in your barn.

To the good old days...we weren't so good,
'cause we weren't so old!

May the Irish hills caress you.
May her lakes and rivers bless you.
May the luck of the Irish enfold you.
May the blessings of St. Patrick behold you.

May the Leprechauns be near you
to spread luck along your way
And may all the Irish angels smile
upon you on St. Pat's Day.

Here's to you,
And here's to me;
But as you're not hear,
Here's two to me.

May you have many children
and may they grow as mature in taste
and healthy in color
and as sought after
as the contents of this glass.

A good wife and health
Are a man's best wealth.

The Triads
of Ireland

Three worst smiles:
  the smile of a wave,
  the smile of a loose woman,
  the grin of a dog ready to leap.

Three things that are best in the world:
  the hand of a good carpenter,
  the hand of a skilled woman,
  the hand of a good smith.

The three wealths of fortunate people:
  a ready conveyance,
  ale without a habitation,
  a safeguard upon the road.

Three sons whom chastity bears to wisdom:
  valor,
  generosity,
  laughter.

Three entertainers of a gathering:
  a jester,
  a juggler,
  a lap-dog.

Three rejoicings followed by sorrow:
  a wooer's,
  a thief's,
  a tale-bearer's.

Three things best for a chief:
  justice,
  peace,
  an army.

Three worst things for a chief:
  sloth,
  treachery,
  evil counsel.

Three rejoicings that are worse than sorrow:
  the joy of a man who has defrauded another,
  the joy of a man who has perjured himself,
  the joy of a man who has slain his brother
  in contesting his land.

The three things that ruin wisdom:
  ignorance,
  inaccurate knowledge,
  forgetfulness.

Three nurses of dignity:
  a fine figure,
  a good memory,
  piety.

Three dark things of the world:
  giving a thing into keeping,
  guaranteeing,
  fostering.

Three unfortunate things for a householder:
  proposing to a bad woman,
  serving a bad chief,
  exchanging for bad land.

Three excellent things for a householder:
  proposing to a good woman,
  serving a good chief,
  exchanging for good land.

Three that are most difficult to talk to:
  a king about his booty,
  a Viking in his hauberk,
  a boor who's under patronage.

Three whose spirits are highest:
  a young scholar after having read his psalms,
  a youngster who has put on a man's attire,
  a maiden who has been made a woman.

Three things which justice demands:
  judgment,
  measure,
  conscience.

Three things which judgment demands:
  wisdom,
  penetration,
  knowledge.

Three wealths in barren places:
  a well in a mountain,
  fire out of a stone,
  wealth in the possession of a hard man.

Three renovators of the world:
  the woman of a woman,
  a cow's udder,
  a smith's molding block.

Three things for which an enemy is loved:
  wealth,
  beauty,
  worth.

Three things for which a friend is hated:
  trespassing,
  keeping aloof,
  fecklessness.

Three concealments upon which forfeiture does not close:
  a wife's dowry,
  the food of a married couple,
  a boy's foster fee.

Three contracts that are reversed by the decision of
a judge:
  the contracts of a woman,
  of a son,
  of a cotter.

Three rude ones of the world:
  a youngster mocking an old man,
  a healthy person mocking an invalid,
  a wise man mocking a fool.

Three that are incapable of special contracts:
  a son whose father is alive,
  a betrothed woman,
  the serf of a chief.

Three sons that do not share inheritance:
  a son begotten in a brake,
  the son of a slave,
  the son of a girl still wearing tresses.

Three sparks that kindle love:
  a face,
  demeanor,
  speech.

Three chains by which evil propensity is bound:
  a covenant,
  a monastic rule,
  law.

The rocks to which lawful behavior is tied:
  a monastery,
  a chieftain,
  the family.

Three deposits with usufruct:
  depositing a woman,
  a horse,
  salt.

Three candles that illumine every darkness:
  truth,
  nature,
  knowledge.

Three glories of the gathering:
  a beautiful wife,
  a good horse,
  a swift hound.

Three things that constitute a king:
  a contract with other kings,
  the feast of Tar,
  abundance during his reign.

Three ungentlemanly things:
  interrupting stories,
  a mischievous game,
  jesting so as to raise a blush.

Three locks that lock up secrets:
  shame,
  silence,
  closeness.

Three smiles that are worse than sorrow:
  the smile of the snow as it melts,
  the smile of your wife on you after another man
  has been with her,
  the grin of a hound ready to leap at you.

Three keys that unlock thoughts:
  drunkenness,
  trustfulness,
  love.

Three fewnesses that are better than plenty:
  a fewness of fine words,
  a fewness of cows in grass,
  a fewness of friends around ale.

Three inheritances that are divided in the presence
of heirs:
  the inheritance of a jester,
  of a madman,
  of an old man.

Three ruins of a tribe:
  a lying chief,
  a false judge,
  a lustful priest.

Three youthful sisters:
  desire,
  beauty,
  generosity.

Three aged sisters:
  groaning,
  chastity,
  ugliness.

Three well-bred sisters:
  constancy,
  well-spokenness
  kindliness.

Three ill-bred sisters:
  fierceness,
  lustfulness,
  obduracy.

Three preparations of a good man's house:
  ale,
  a bath,
  a large fire.

Three characteristics of obstinacy:
  long visits,
  staring,
  constant questioning.

Three sisters of good fortune:
  good breeding,
  liberality,
  mirth.

The three chief sins:
  avarice,
  gluttony,
  lust.

Three sisters of good repute:
  diligence,
  prudence,
  bountifulness.

Three sisters of ill repute:
  inertness,
  grudging,
  close-fistedness.

The things that constitute a harper:
  a tune to make you cry,
  a tune to make you laugh,
  a tune to put you to sleep.

Three angry sisters:
  blasphemy,
  strife,
  foulmouthedness.

Three irreverent sisters:
  usefulness,
  an easy bearing,
  firmness.

Three sounds of increase:
  the lowing of a cow in milk,
  the din of a smithy,
  the swish of a plow.

Three causes that do not die with neglect:
  the causes of an imbecile,
  of oppression,
  of ignorance.

Three bloodsheds that need not be impunged:
  the bloodshed of battle,
  of jealousy,
  of mediating.

Three things by which every angry person is known:
  an outburst of passion,
  trembling,
  growing pale.

Three things that characterize every patient person:
  repose,
  silence,
  blushing.

Three cohabitations that do not pay a marriage-portion:
  taking her by force,
  outraging her without her knowledge through drunkenness,
  her being violated by a king.

Three that are not entitled to exemption:
    restoring a son,
    the tools of an artificer,
    hostageship.

Three signs of folly:
    contention,
    wrangling,
    attachment to everybody.

Three deposits that need not be returned:
    the deposits of an imbecile,
    of a high dignitary,
    a fixed deposit.

Three dead ones that are paid for with living things:
    an apple tree,
    a hazel bush,
    a sacred grove.

Three things that make a fool wise:
    learning,
    steadiness,
    docility.

Three things that neither swear nor are sworn:
    a woman,
    a son who does not support his father,
    a dumb person.

Three things that make a wise man foolish:
  quarreling,
  anger,
  drunkenness.

Three that are not entitled to renunciation of authority:
  a son and his father,
  a wife and her husband,
  a serf and his lord.

Three things that show every good man:
  a special gift,
  valor,
  piety.

Three things that show a bad man:
  bitterness,
  hatred,
  cowardice.

Three who do not adjudicate though they are possessed of wisdom:
  a man who sues,
  a man who is being sued,
  a man who is bribed to give judgment.

Three on whom acknowledgment does not fall in its time:
  death,
  ignorance,
  carelessness.

Three great rushes:
  the rush of water,
  the rush of fire,
  the rush of falsehood.

Three maidens that bring hatred upon misfortune:
  talking,
  laziness,
  insincerity.

Three maidens that bring love to good fortune:
  silence,
  diligence,
  sincerity.

Three woman-days:
  Monday,
  Tuesday,
  Wednesday.

Three man-days:
  Thursday,
  Friday,
  Sunday.

Three hateful things in speech:
  stiffness,
  obscurity,
  a bad delivery.

The three finest sights in the world:
    a field of ripe wheat,
    a ship in full sail,
    the wife of a MacDonnell with child.

Three things that are undignified for everyone:
    driving one's horse before one's lord so as to soil
    his dress,
    going to speak to him without being summoned,
    staring in his face as he is eating his food.

Three steadinesses of good womanhood:
    keeping a steady tongue,
    a steady chastity,
    a steady housewifery.

Three welcomes of an ale-house:
    plenty,
    kindliness,
    art.

Three prohibitions of food:
    to eat it without giving thanks,
    to eat it before its proper time,
    to eat it after a guest.

Three excellences of dress:
    elegance,
    comfort,
    lastingness.

Three indications of a dignity in a person:
 a fine figure,
 a fine bearing,
 eloquence.

Three that are not entitled to sick-maintenance:
 a man who absconds from his chief,
 from his family,
 from his poet.

Three coffers whose depth is not known:
 the coffer of a chieftain,
 of the Church,
 of a privileged poet.

Three disagreeable things at home:
 a scolding wife,
 a squalling child,
 a smoky chimney.

Your Own Pages for Personal Notes and Cocktails